MW00711713

The Saga of

DEAD-EYE

BOOK ONE:
VAMPIRES, ZOMBIES,
& MOJO MEN

Ronald Kelly

1/9/22

The Saga of
DEAD-EYE

BOOK ONE:
VAMPIRES, ZOMBIES, & MOJO MEN

by

RONALD KELLY

www.silvershamrockpublishing.com

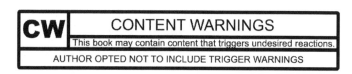

Copyright © 2021 Ronald Kelly

Front Cover Artwork by Alex McVey
Front Cover Design by Zach McCain/Kenneth W. Cain
Interior art by Ronald Kelly
Formatted by Kenneth W. Cain
Edited by Kenneth W. Cain

Book One: Vampires, Zombies, & Mojo Men
is dedicated to the following folks:

Nicholas Gray
Ruthann Jagge
Marina Schnierer
Deb Soward
and
Bridgett Nelson

INTRODUCTION

As you begin your journey through the weird and wicked territory of the Old West in *The Saga of Dead-Eye*, you may be thinking "It looks like Ol' Ron has finally decided to jump on the Splatter Western bandwagon."

Well...not exactly.

The character of Dead-Eye has been around for quite a while. It originated way back in 1976, at the end of my junior year in high school. I was an aspiring comic book artist then and hadn't yet gotten bitten by the fiction-writing bug. A fellow classmate, Lowell Cunningham, and I had done several amateur comic books together, namely titles like *Ka: Son of Ra*, a superhero based on the bird-headed Egyptian deity, and *Wolf*, a covert spy/ninja with silver hair and a bo staff. By that point, I had created a number of superheroes of my own: the deadly Adversary, the scientific mash-up of frog and man, Amphibi-Human, the laser-shooting/unbreakable Glassman, the Rebel, a faceless motorcycle hero with a Southern-fried twist, and an Aquaman-like pulp hero of the 1930s (my homage to Doc Savage and the Avenger) named the Piranha. And then there was another one called Dead-Eye. The western gunfighter with the glowing left eye never made it into one of my hand-drawn comic books, but it intrigued me to create such a character, mainly because I was beginning to read more and more western literature at that time, by authors such as Zane Gray, Charles Portis, and Louis L'Amour.

About mid-way through my senior year, I had decided to spend less time on comic book drawing and creating, and devote the lion's share of my efforts on writing short stories. Dead-Eye and the other heroes were shuffled into a binder and confined to dark oblivion in my mother's old cedar chest. After graduation, I knew that I wanted to be a published author and the long and relentless process of teaching myself that craft through trial and error began. My friend, Lowell, pursued his comic book aspirations and eventually sold a comic series called *The Men in Black* to Aircel Comics (later acquired by Malibu), and we all know what that led to cinematically.

I wandered from one genre of fiction to another (science fiction, men's adventure, mystery/noir, etc.) and finally settled on writing traditional western novels around 1981. I initially wrote two short novels, *The Battle of Reb Bowen* (which was misplaced and completely lost during my ten year hiatus from writing) and *Timber Gray* (which was eventually published by Thunderstorm Books as a limited edition Douglas Western in 2011, then later in paperback by Bad Moon Books, and currently in e-book and audiobook from Crossroad Press). In 1983, I set on an ambitious writing journey that spanned a grueling two years in length. After reading Brian Garfield's 477 page door-stopper western novel, *Wild Times,* I decided to revive Dead-Eye in a lavish western odyssey through the Old West and make my mark as a published author in that manner. As it turned out, *The Saga of Dead-Eye* became something of an obsession during the writing process and reached a bloated, overindulgent 880 type-written pages. Needless to say, my agent was unwilling to submit such an ambitious (and, yes, I admit, crudely plotted and written) tome to the western publishers, when they were accustomed to releasing quick-reads of 120 to 150 pages. So, once again, Dead-Eye was shuffled back to the dark tomb of the cedar chest. In 1986, I found my literary niche in the horror genre and began to publish short fiction in small press magazines like *Cemetery Dance, Deathrealm,* and *Eldritch Tales,* which, in turn, aced me a six-year run of Southern-Fried horror novels with mass market publisher, Zebra Books.

As I settled into the first leg of my career as a horror author (1986 through 1996), I began to read whatever horror western fiction was available at the time; works like Joe R. Lansdale's *The Magic Wagon,* Dirck Van Sickle's *Montana Gothic,* and the Dark Harvest anthology *Razored Saddles.* During my horror writing stretch with Zebra, I acquired a sweet (but short) gig with Berkley Books in 1993, ghostwriting for the Jake Logan western series. That went away after only two books on my part (#174 *Slocum and the Nightriders* and #187 *Slocum and the Gold Slaves),* but I still had a hankering to do some western work. That was when Ol' Dead-Eye sat up in his cedar casket and said, "Want to give it another try, partner?"

So, my agent pitched a *Dead-Eye* horror-western series to Berkley. This time Dead-Eye would be a zombie gunfighter and roam the Old West battling a different monster in every book. Now, zombies were hardly even a thing in the horror genre back in 1994 (and wouldn't be until Brian Keene's *The Rising* and Image Comics' *The Walking Dead* around 2003), so I'd say if anything inspired my idea it was probably *Dead in the West,* Joe Lansdale's short novel of a zombie apocalypse in a small Texas town. Berkley Books considered my pitch, but unfortunately, didn't accept it. They didn't believe that I could sustain a long-running western series (at least 200-plus books according to their business strategy) with a 'monster of the month' formula. I was disappointed by the rejection, but knew they were probably right. After Dead-Eye had fought all the traditional monsters like vampires, werewolves, and ghosts, he would have lapsed into forced absurdity and ended up taking on Bigfoot, the Loch Ness Monster, and little gray aliens from UFOs. And there was no way I was going to take him down that path.

So, back into the chest he went. And there he stayed...until 2020...the year COVID-19 struck.

That was when Texas-based Death's Head Press published Wile E. Young's *The Magpie Coffin* and the sub-genre known as Splatter Western was born. As DHP issued one incredibly creepy western after another, my interest was piqued and Dead-Eye came to mind once again. So, I decided to dust him off and pair him with a Louisiana mojo man sidekick by the name of Job, and send them in pursuit of the vampire Jules Holland and his outlaw band of demonic minions, including the evil enchantress, Evangeline. I pitched the concept for publication consideration once again and, thankfully, it was welcomed with open arms. I'm very pleased to have Silver Shamrock presenting *The Saga of Dead-Eye* in its entirety after all this time.

You currently hold Book One of *Dead-Eye*'s intended five volume run in your hands. You'll discover a mixed saddlebag here: straight horror, black humor, fantasy, historic fiction, and maybe even some cosmic horror thanks to the mysterious Hole Out of Nowhere. You'll be crossing paths with some classic monsters and cryptids along the way, as well as new creatures from other worlds and realms. There will even be supporting characters from the RK mythos showing up from time to time. This first offering, *Vampires, Zombie, & Mojo Men*, includes some familiar visitors from works like *Fear, After the Burn,* and my novella, *Strong Steps*.

So, here we are. Finally, after languishing in creative limbo for nigh onto forty-five years, Dead-Eye rides the dark trail, armed with his trusty .44 Dragoon, a ghastly glowing eye that strikes terror in the dead of night, and an almighty thirst for vengeance that can't be quenched, even by the finality of death itself. You are invited to saddle up your hoss and go along, too. But be sure to pack your wooden stakes and silver bullets before we head out, and maybe even a mojo hand or chicken foot or two…

Many Happy Nightmares!
Ronald Kelly
Brush Creek, Tennessee
August 2021

CHAPTER ONE

Pine City, California
August 1878

They put a single bullet in the head of the bartender; a forty-four caliber slug two inches above the bushy brow of his left eye. The man—known only to them as Wallace for the past three days of their stay in Pine City—stumbled back a couple of steps and blinked a time or two, as though he had been bee-stung, rather than shot point-blank in the skull. It took a moment before his addled senses caught up with his mangled brain. He was a big, burly man, so when he finally gave up the ghost and went down, he went down hard. Liquor bottles and glass beer mugs rattled and clinked as he hit the hardwood floor.

Other than Arkansas Bob Penny and Dale Sloat, Wallace had been the last man alive in the saloon. There had been six others, but they lay about the barroom in various degrees of physical ruin and decay. Some had been shot down, while others had been carved and gutted by the foot-long blade of Bob's Arkansas Toothpick. At least two still wore the brass stars of the town marshal and his deputy. The place stank like a slaughterhouse, but the two gunmen breathed it in with cruel relish and satisfaction, for it was the scent of violence begat of freedom. They had been five weeks away from Yuma—that boiling shithole of a territorial prison—and had vented two years' worth of pent-up rage on every town they had rode through, from New Mexico to Nevada to the flourishing greenness of California beyond the hot sands of Death Valley.

Laughing, the two burst from the shadows of the drinking establishment into the brilliant sunlight and staggered into the dusty street beyond the boardwalk. Dale—a lean, bearded man with a deep scar running the length of his ugly face from scalp to chin—held half a bottle of rye whiskey in one hand and a Remington Army revolver in the other; the one he had stolen off the body of a gut shot cattleman who had been taking his herd to market near Araz Junction.

Arkansas Bob wore a brace of Schofield pistols and the big hunting knife on his belt. He was as adept with the guns as a blacksmith with a mallet or a muleskinner with a bullwhip. Even blind drunk, the tall, broad-shouldered man with the muttonchop whiskers could place his shot within an inch of his intended aim, nine times out of ten.

Down the street echoed the continuous strike of a hammer on tenpenny nails. The town undertaker worked diligently to catch up with his casket-building. Seven had been buried already. Counting those in the saloon and several who lay in the street, bloated and ripe, twelve more would be measured and fitted for a pine box and buried in the rocky earth of the cemetery south of the town limits. Thanks to Bob and Dale, he had been a mighty busy man.

"What now?" asked Dale, bored and at a loss of something to do. "Women?"

"A horny bastard, you are," chuckled Bob. "You've straddled pert near every gal in this town, whether they be willing or not. All that's left is the pastor's cross-legged wife and that dried-up, old spinster of a schoolmarm."

"Tell you what. We'll flip a coin," suggested the other. "Just to see who gets the pick of the two."

As they stood there, allowing their eyes to grow accustomed to the noonday sun and fumbling for a double eagle with which to do their wagering, their gaze was suddenly drawn to the train depot across the street; the only stop the Pacific Railroad made for fifty miles, east or west, of Pine City.

The platform opposite the tracks was deserted...except for a single, lone form. A tall, rawboned man dressed in a black broadcloth suit and low-crowned hat, sitting on a bench. His arms looked stiff, the fingers of the pale hands curled inward to the palms, and his long legs were splayed and stretched forward, the heels of his boots resting upon the dusty boards.

They could smell the godawful stench from where they stood. They knew the odor and appearance of a dead man when they saw one.

"What do you make of it, Bob?" Dale asked his partner. "Someone leaving such...just sitting there, stinking like hell and drawing flies?"

"Weren't one that we did," claimed the other. "I would've recalled a high-dressed dandy like that."

They took a few steps closer. From the shadow beneath the cadaver's hat-brim, a long, pale face could be seen. The stubbled cheeks were sunken and hollow, as were the dark sockets around the eyes. One of the orbs was closed—eternally so, they were certain— while the left eye was wide open. The white of it was tainted a pale yellow in color and glowed oddly, like foxfire, in the gloom cast by the hat. A broad, black mustache graced his upper lip and, just below the right cheekbone, the flesh had split open. Inside the laceration, maggots writhed and squirmed. Some had liberated themselves from the wound and crawled along the slope of his jaw toward the chin and the cold, blue lips just above.

"I reckon he ain't got no purpose in being there," Dale said. He grinned with rotten, tobacco-stained teeth and lifted the Remington at arm's length. "Excepting maybe for target practice." He took a long swig from the bottle, then thumbed back the hammer, steadied his aim, and fired.

The revolver bucked like a mule kick in his hand. Amid the bluish cloud of gun smoke, a forty-four slug nailed a pearl button just below the corpse's string tie; the kind worn by riverboat gamblers or plantation owners, before the War Between the States had laid their pride and livelihood low with sorrow and humiliation. In the button's place was a hole as big as the plug of a man's thumb. As they expected, what little blood did manage to surface seeped as a thick, dark sludge and not the bright and jetting current that a living man would produce if shot in such a place.

"My turn now," said Bob. He drew both of the Schofields and unleashed two shots, one after the other. Two more buttons were driven deep into the torso of the carcass, one just below the breastbone and the other further down, above his navel.

"I think I'm gonna put this one square betwixt his eyes," Dale told his partner. He laid the ball of his thumb across the spur of the hammer, intending to cycle the cylinder until a fresh round positioned itself, primed and ready. But, before he could cock the pistol, something peculiar happened.

The dead man slowly opened his right eye—steel gray and bloodshot—and looked straight at them.

Stunned, they watched as he rose from where he sat on the bench. As he did so, his joints crackled and his stiffening muscles and tendons creaked like old leather weathered by sun and harsh elements. The cadaver glared at them for a long moment, then looked down and regarded the bullet holes in his chest.

"Well I'll be damned," he said with a Southern drawl. His voice was deep and hollow, like the echo from an empty and waterless well. "That was my favorite shirt."

Arkansas Bob and Dale looked from his frowning face to the gun belt buckled around his narrow hips. He wore only one pistol—a big Colt Dragoon .44—holstered across his belly from the left, the curved butt of polished ivory jutting toward the right for a cross-draw. Fortunately, though, the man's gaunt hand, pale and bloodless, was held limply along his right thigh, as if having no intention of moving.

They looked at one another and laughed, intending to aim their guns and fire. But they never received the chance.

Arkansas Bob had once seen a rattlesnake strike from a few feet away.

When he had been a younger man, working with his pa in the tobacco fields back home in Arkansas, he had stepped out of one row into another. A rattler, its buttons buzzing menacingly, had sat coiled in the dirt, a yard away. One second, it had simply been resting there, while in the flash of another, its triangular head had hit the toe of his boot forcefully, burying its fangs deeply into the leather. The strike had been so swift that his eyes had been unable to comprehend it.

That was how it was with the dead man on the depot platform. One moment, his hand was lank and limp by his side, while the next it was full of deadly steel and ear-splitting fury. The Dragoon was a fine piece of work; rechambered for .44 cartridges and nickel-plated with fancy scrolled engraving on the cylinder and barrel. The slug caught Dale on the tip of his nose, splitting flesh and cartilage, burrowing past the tender membrane of his sinuses and tearing through the base of his brain. The outlaw didn't even have a chance to cock the Remington's hammer half way before he was on his back in the street, his brains and blood pooling in the dirt beneath him.

"Oh, shit!" said Bob, unaware that he had uttered the last words of his cruel and pointless life. Before he could even lift the brace of

Schofields into line, the dead man fanned the Colt's hammer twice. Two slugs left the muzzle with the boom of one, striking the pupils of his eyes and bursting them into spurting streamers of colorless jelly. The bullets tunneled past the occipital bones of his sockets and into the tissue of his brainpan. They converged when they reached the back of his skull, taking away a chunk of bone and flap of scalp the size of a man's fist.

Arkansas Bob Penny fell and lay beside Dale Sloat, as dead as those they had murdered and abandoned in a dozen little towns during their murderous rampage across the western territory.

"Shitfire!" exclaimed a voice from the boardwalk across the street. "Can't I even run an errand or two without you up and misbehaving?"

The gunfighter with the glowing yellow eye returned his revolver to its holster and regarded the one who spoke. "Blowing a man's buttons off and punching him full of holes while he's napping deserves an equal measure, in my opinion. You aiming to argue the point?"

The fellow—a short, bald negro with a dusty derby hat and a picket of silver and gold teeth—crossed the street with several wrapped parcels held in his lean arms. "No sir, not me. From what I've heard, they were aiming to make the undertaker yonder a rich man. I'd say that mortician will likely have these two bastards propped up in their caskets for photos and such, charging a dime a head for the pleasure of posing with 'em and spitting in their faces. Then, after he's drawn all the coin he can, he'll dump their sorry carcasses in a dry wash and let the buzzards and bugs have their turn."

"Serves them right," said the dead man, "for desecrating a man's garment in such a callus and thoughtless manner."

"Is that what's put a burr between your balls? Your confounded shirt?"

"Wanted to look presentable...for our train ride to San Francisco," was all he had to say in reply.

The other shook his head in exasperation. "Aw, hell! I'll go back to the store and buy you another, if it'll stop your bitching and moaning." Then, cussing beneath his breath, the old man dumped his parcels on the bench in disgust and crossed the street, heading toward the mercantile he had just come from. "Sure got your hosses hitched to a wagonload of vanity, particularly for a flyblown son of a bitch like you."

The long and lanky gunfighter known only as Dead-Eye looked down at his chest. He probed at the bullet hole below his breastbone. Curiously, he stuck his index finger in, up to the middle knuckle. When he withdrew it, the digit was nearly dry. He sighed, wiped what little refuse that was there on his ruined shirtfront, and sat back down on the bench. He resumed the position he had been in before, pulled his hat brim low, and closed his only good eye. The other remained open, glowing dully and blindly in the shadows.

As his thoughts drifted to slumber, he considered his plight. How long had they traveled together...he and the black man? Days...months...years? A decade or more? It was hard to recall, even though the reason for doing so was always there, foremost in his cold, worm-eaten brain, like the white-hot tip of a branding iron against tender flesh.

After all, the ticking of time was lost on the dead...even those eager to settle a score.

CHAPTER TWO

Athens, Georgia
September 1866

Devastation and ruin. The acrid stench of ash and scorched stone. Windows devoid of glass; dark, with nary a lamp or lantern to guide him home. That was what welcomed Joshua Wingade as he reined his black Morgan toward the two-story mansion. On either side of the lane were the towering magnolia trees that had once stood like sentries, majestic and full. Now they were black...not from flame, but as though each and every one had been stricken by some awful, poisonous blight. Their thick leaves were dark and discolored; as ebony as coal, mottled with thick veins of putrid violet.

Joshua surveyed the state of the plantation, feeling overwhelmed by what had become of his childhood home. He brought his horse to a halt and paused to collect himself. Beneath the brass buttons of his slate gray uniform, which was stained and torn, his heart raced swiftly, driving him toward panic. The tall, lean man with the pitch black hair and broad mustache closed his gray eyes and breathed deeply, attempting to calm himself. After a long moment, he felt able to proceed. He unbuttoned the flap on his side holster and uncovered the walnut grip of his Leech & Rigdon 36-caliber pistol. The revolver was a poor Confederate imitation of the Union's Colt Navy; less accurate and notoriously undependable. Joshua was knowledgeable of such things, for he had once been proficient with guns, be it pistol or long rifle. But the conflict between the North and the South, all that he had experienced during those four dire and dreadful years, had cruelly robbed him of that skill.

He rode onward. The bruised and bloody hues of that evening's sunset marred the Georgia sky like ugly and incurable wounds. The long shadows of dusk stretched across the grounds of the plantation and embraced the towering structure of the manor house. The closer he drew, the stronger his apprehension became. When he reached the front of the mansion, Joshua dismounted and struggled to tie the horse's reins to an iron hitching post. The lengths of leather jittered in his trembling hands.

Damned war, he thought bitterly, attempting to steady himself.

Hesitantly, the man stood at the bottom steps and regarded the fire-burnished columns and the double doors of heavy oak, which now stood splintered and askew on their hinges. The house's entranceway was as dark and inviting as the mouth of a cave. Mounting the stairs to the long porch, he shucked the revolver from its sheath. The steel of the gun rattled in his hand as his nerves betrayed him.

Joshua stepped through the gaping doorway, into the vestibule beyond. Gloom and desolation was all that he encountered. Whatever had not been stolen had been turned into refuse and wreckage. He looked toward the grand staircase that gave access to the floor of rooms above. No light shown from the upper level as well. It was as though the entire place was deserted…as though no one was there at all.

"Elizabeth?" he called out in alarm. "Daniel?"

At first, there came no reply. His deep voice rang through empty chambers and halls, resounding almost jarringly so, then falling silent.

Then, abruptly, a voice spoke out, startling him. "Who goes there?" There was raw fear in the man's tone. "Reveal yourself or, so help me God, I'll shoot you dead!"

Joshua stared at the open doorway of the manor's grand ballroom; where formal balls and lavish gatherings had been held with great fanfare during happier days. A faint glow emanated from within. Holding the pistol ahead of him, he warily stepped inside. There was a low fire burning in the big marble fireplace at the far end of the room. Before it, hunkered a lone form, small and sunken with age and defeat.

"I am Major Joshua Wingade of Anderson's 5th Calvary," he called out. "Who are you, sir, and what business do you have here?"

The dark figure seemed relieved. "It's just me, Mister Josh," he replied with a voice that was coarse, yet familiar.

Joshua holstered his revolver and started toward the hearth. "George? Is that you?"

"Yessir…or whatever's left of me."

When he got halfway across the ballroom, Joshua was surprised to find that the elderly negro was surrounded by a half-circle consisting of a dozen crosses. All were crudely constructed from the broken frames of the guest chairs that had once stood along the walls and encircled the elegant dance floor. "What is the meaning of this, George? And what, in God's holy name, took place here?"

"Come within this circle and we will talk," said the other. "If you cannot, I will know that you are not the man you once were. Or even a man at all."

Joshua stepped past two of the makeshift crucifixes and regarded the old gentleman who sat there. George had been his father's personal servant until the patriarch's death from pneumonia three years into the conflict. Despite President Lincoln's Proclamation, he had stayed on to watch over the remainder of the Wingade family. The black man sported a wooly gray beard and a dark face full of sorrow and suspicion. His right leg appeared to be broken. It was splinted with two chair legs and bound in strips of red velvet material from the ballroom drapes. George held a double-barreled shotgun across his lap. The Confederate officer recognized the firearm. The twelve-gauge scattergun had been special made for Joshua's father, Elias, by Henri Pieper of Liege, Belgium. The scattergun sported twin barrels of blued Damascus steel and curved hammers behind the percussion port of each breach.

Its muzzles had been directed unerringly toward the rebel officer before he had entered the circle of crosses. They now drooped toward the floor for, in Old George's mind, he no longer posed a threat.

"Where in tarnation have you been, Mister Josh?" the elderly man asked. "It's been well over a year since the War ended. We thought you were long dead."

"Some days it seemed worse than death," the tall, mustachioed man admitted truthfully. "I was confined in a Union prison camp since the spring of '63, taken prisoner at Franklin in Tennessee. Camp Chase in Ohio, a particular vile and tortuous place. I was only released two months ago. Given a horse and my sidearm, and told to go home."

George noticed how haggard and gaunt the man appeared, how his hands trembled involuntarily, as if with a palsy. "Good Lord, son…what's happened to you?"

"Battle upon ugly battle…it wore me down, George…shattered my nerves. The report of cannon fire, the crack of the rifles, the awful screams of the horribly wounded and dying. It changed me…filled me with shame and despair…made me less of the man that I was before. That and the cruel depravity I suffered within the walls of the stockade. Disease and starvation…chained and cruelly beaten like I were nothing more than a wild animal."

"Bloodshed and ruination can break one's spirit," agreed the old man. "You were a kind and gentle man. Moody and down in the mouth at times, but still a good one who never should have been forced by honor to fight in that hellacious war...particularly for a cause I know you despised with every ounce of your soul."

"A greater truth has never been spoken," the tall man said. Joshua's thoughts turned away from the past and focused on the present. "So, tell me...what happened here?" he asked, although he feared the answer he might receive.

"Hell came to call," George told him sternly. "And stayed for a day or two. Long enough to destroy all that was good and sacred about this place."

Joshua stood next to the hearth and faced the elderly man. "Was it the Union?"

George shook his head. "No, this took place scarcely a week ago. We thought they were bushwhackers at first, but they were outlaws instead. Not of the common sort, however. These were spawned of brimstone and hellfire...as though Purgatory had cracked open and spewed them out."

"I don't understand..."

Nervously, George stared through the shattered panes of one of the ballroom windows. The sunset had darkened, its colors deepening toward twilight. "Listen to me carefully and you shall. Remember those stories I once told you at bedtime? When you were a small child?"

Joshua nodded. "The tales that gave me nightmares. The ones about ghosts, goblins, and..."

"Vampires," clarified Old George. "The leader of the lot—the one called Jules Holland—that was what he was, as sure as I live and breathe. A cultured man of noble upbringing, but pale of flesh and with eyes as red as freshly-let blood. Those with him were spawned of other evils...demons and creatures conjured from black magic. There was a woman with them as well… a witch of my color who did Holland's bidding. She consumed this place with black fire and cursed every growing thing that flourished upon the property."

"And my family?" Joshua demanded. "Dear Elizabeth and young Daniel?"

A strange expression crossed the black man's wrinkled face. "Your wife was taken by the lot and violated, time and time again. Sweet Lord in Heaven, how her screams of pain and humiliation rang throughout this structure. Then the vampire Holland, he feasted upon her. Drained every last drop of blood from her ravaged body. When they left, they took the child with them…for what purpose, I have no earthly notion."

Joshua stumbled backward and steadied himself with one of the makeshift crosses. His mind struggled with what George had told him. "And you did nothing to defend them?"

"I tried, Mister Josh… I swear to God I did. But one of the bandits…a giant of a man named Boar…nearly killed me. He took hold of me as though I had no more weight than a rag doll and threw me against the marble hearth, shattering the bones of my leg. They would have surely done me in, if it hadn't been for this." He took hold of a length of rawhide around his neck and drew it from his shirt. Secured to its end was a small cross carved of soft pine. "The sign of the crucifixion held them at bay. It was like a poison to them. They abandoned me…afraid to look upon it."

"Elizabeth…where is she now?" Joshua wanted to know.

George was silent for a long moment. He glanced toward the ballroom window once again. "Despite my infirmity, I managed to drag her outside and bury her in the flower garden that she loved so dearly. It was a difficult and lengthy task, but one I knew she was deserving of."

Joshua took a hesitant step toward the window.

"But she's there no longer," the old man told him grimly. "She...she clawed her way out of the earth, Mister Josh. Stepped up into the darkness of night and laughed with a black humor and delight that is not of this world. She came looking for me...to feed...but couldn't bring herself to approach." He nodded toward the barrier of crosses that surrounded him. "She was repelled by what she found here...but she comes nightly and taunts me, attempting to lure me from my stronghold with the promise of food and water. Sometimes she tempts with a great banquet that stands at the far side of the hall...but one that has only been conjured in my mind. I've stayed strong, though. I haven't given in yet...haven't taken the bait. I'd rather starve and perish, than share the evil that she has been cursed with."

It was unfathomable to believe of such things, but Joshua saw by the fear and sorrow in the man's eyes that what he said was the truth. "Where is she now?"

"In the cellar. She sleeps there in daylight. But she will soon stir and roam the house again. As soon as dusk deepens and the sun is gone, she'll be on the prowl." He regarded Joshua sternly. "It's up to you, Mister Josh. Up to you to deal with her. If not with courage, then with mercy. She's your beloved. You'd not want her to carry this burden for eternity, would you?"

Dread settled in the pit of Joshua like a cold and heavy stone. "No," he admitted. He absently laid his right hand on the curved butt of the cap and ball pistol.

"That'll do you no good at all," George told him. He reached toward the flagstones of the hearth and handed him something. It was one of the broken chair legs. Its end had been carved to a wicked point. "I had a hand in making these chairs and I know what manner of tree the wood came from. Pure ash from the woods south of the cotton fields."

Joshua took the length of wood and held it in both hands. It shook and shuddered in his unsettled grasp. "I don't want to go down there," he said, his voice as weak and shaken as his constitution.

"I know, son. But you have no choice. It must be done."

The tall man nodded and tightened his grip on the chair leg. Then, bracing himself, he left the ballroom and headed for the door beneath the big staircase. The one that led to the dank and shadowy depths of the cellar below. One by one, Joshua Wingade descended the wooden risers of the steps, leaving the door open behind him. In the waning light, he found a coal oil lantern hanging from a rafter overhead. Taking a sulfur match from his trouser pocket, he struck it, lifted the glass chimney, and lit the wick. Low, muted light illuminated the basement.

At first, all he saw was the bare, stone walls of the house's foundation, along with kegs of wine and whiskey, and some old furniture that had been stored there many years ago. The floor of the cellar consisted of bare earth. He noticed that a hollow had been scooped away in the center of the room. One roughly five and a half feet by three.

"It is my bed," a woman's voice whispered from a corner choked in shadow.

Joshua stood stone still, afraid to move.

"Elizabeth?" His voice echoed hoarsely through the broad chamber.

"Yes...it is I. Come to me, my love. Surrender and we shall lie there, and consummate your new life within the embrace of the grave."

Joshua's heart beat wildly. He attempted to hold the length of sharpened ash steadily before him, but it wavered nervously in the glow of the lantern. "Life? If what George has told me is truth, life has nothing to do with what you are now."

"I hate to admit it, but the old bastard is correct," she said, stepping into the flickering light. "This may not be life...not *true* life...but it is glorious and redeeming, nevertheless. Join me, dear Joshua, and we shall walk the night, hand in hand."

Elizabeth was every bit as beautiful as she had been five years earlier, before the War Between the States had wrenched him violently from the bosom of his family. But her beauty was not a natural and healthy one. Her skin was as pale as a garden grub and her golden hair was tangled and littered with dirt and debris. Her green eyes burned hungrily in the shadowy pits of their sockets and her lips looked dark, more bruised than crimson. Her slender neck bore the ugly wounds of the attack that had robbed her of goodness and decency, and replaced those blessings with damnation. Two puckered holes above the artery where the one named Holland had suckled until her heart grew still and her veins lay fallow and dry. She was dressed in a nightgown of delicate, white silk; the one he had purchased during a trip to Atlanta shortly after their marriage vows had been uttered and they had become man and wife. The apparel was smeared with fresh earth and splatters of blood...more a shroud than a garment intended for the living.

"You know very well that you are not going to leave this cellar unchanged," she told him slyly. The woman walked slowly, deliberately, encircling him like a cat on the prowl. "I can promise you that."

"What has happened to you?" he asked, attempting to conceal his fright. "You're no longer the woman I remember...the kind and gentle wife, the loving mother of our child."

Elizabeth laughed. It was an ugly sound, that echoed eerily in his thoughts as well as his ears. "Immortality is remarkably liberating, husband. No more worry or strife. No paralyzing fear or insecurity. Simply boldness and a sense of superiority among those poor souls who travel through their scant allotment of years, mundane and weak of backbone and spirit. You, dear Joshua, have always suffered from those inadequacies rather plentifully. Becoming like me should do you a world of good."

"You were always a quiet and demure woman, blessed with humility," he told her. "It seems like this newfound state of yours has hinged your tongue in the middle."

"Then, by all means, let us dispense with my idle talk."

Startled, he watched as she moved toward him at incredible speed, almost as though her feet scarcely touched the earthen floor. An instant later, she was standing before him. Elizabeth's hand struck with a force that knocked him completely off his feet. He somersaulted, head over heels, and crashed into a sturdy timber support that braced the floor above. With a groan, he slid to the floor. He fought the pain of the impact and, using the chair leg as a crutch, attempted to regain his feet.

Again, she was upon him…this time from behind. He felt an icy hand upon the back of his neck, tightening, forcefully wrenching his head around. With a hiss that could only be described as feline in nature, she lowered her head to the column of this throat. Joshua felt something wickedly sharp prick his flesh and he lashed backward with the length of wood. It struck her in the ribs, causing her to release him with a gasp.

The man stumbled into the center of the cellar and faced her, holding the pike of the chair leg before him to keep her at bay.

Elizabeth smiled, bearing sharp, white teeth with cuspids as long as his index finger. "Let me show you the trickery I have learnt since my turning," she boasted. And, with that, she faded into a form of dense shadow that gradually diminished in size and mass. At the same instant something flew toward him, swooping toward his head. It was a small, gray bat. As the winged creature encircled his head, Joshua could hear her laughter in his mind, joyous and taunting. He attempted to strike the bat, but it alluded his efforts.

"Not of your liking?" her voice rang through the cellar. "How about this then?" Suddenly, the timbered ceiling and the earth of the floor were covered with a skittering mass of small black spiders…black widows from the looks of them.

Just as quickly, the legion dissolved into nothingness and her voice sounded directly behind him. "Or rather this?"

Joshua whirled just as a large rat launched itself from an overhead beam. Out of defense, he swung the chair leg and, by chance, batted it away from him. Stunned, the rodent tumbled across the basement floor. Before it could recover, he brought the point of the length of ash downward, impaling the squirming creature. Elizabeth's screams of defeat cut through his brain like broken shards of glass. He watched in horror as the rat disseminated and, in its place, writhed the body of his beloved. The whittled point of the chair leg had been driven through the sternum of her ribcage and pierced her heart.

Eyes as red as newly let blood glared at him accusingly. "You refuse my gift?" she shrieked. "After having made such an alluring appeal?"

"Your invitation was wasted in breath, dear one," he said, his gray eyes brimming with tears. "There is nothing enticing about the thing you have become."

With all his weight, he drove the stake deeper until the sack of her heart was torn apart. A gorge of blood bubbled from her throat and spilled past her dark lips, staining her alabaster cheeks and chin with rivulets of crimson. "You are lost. All that is left is saving is our son from those scoundrels."

She reached up and grasped at the folds of his uniform. Her fingers were weak, faltering. For a moment, the fury in her eyes abated and the woman he had loved was present once again. "Don't do it, Josh. If you pursue them, they will kill you…or leave you as they left me. Jules Holland is ruthless…a fiend! And those who ride with him…they are not of our world. They are of a time and realm beyond the creations of Genesis. From a place that makes Hell seem tame and pleasurable in comparison."

"Perhaps so," he told her. "But I must at least try."

"Then, God go with you. And may He have mercy on your soul." And, with that blessing, his sweet Elizabeth lost substance, changing first into shadow, then ebbing into nothingness. Shocked, he found the sharpened point of the chair leg anchored deeply in the earth of the cellar floor.

For a fleeting moment, Joshua Wingade felt her breath upon his face and the tender petals of her lips pressed upon his own...then she was forever gone.

The following morning, as the pale, gray light of dawn shone through the tall windows of the ballroom, George sat before the hearth. He warmed his aged bones and partook of water and food that Wingade had brought to him from the saddlebags of the Morgan.

When the tall man appeared in the open doorway, George was surprised. He was dressed in a shirt of white silk, black string tie, dark britches, and a long, black broadcloth coat. His head sported a low-crowned black hat.

"Doesn't look much like traveling clothes," the black man observed.

"This was all I could manage to find," Joshua told him. "I never was much of a traveling man before...not until the War took me here, there, and yonder."

George smiled. "Well, you always were something of a dandy, if you ask me. What became of the uniform?"

The tall man's face darkened. "I set it afire on the back veranda. I'm rid of it and the sorrow it brought about."

"All for the best, I suppose." The old man studied him for a moment. "Come here. I've got something for you."

When Joshua had crossed the ballroom, George reached beneath his chair and produced a gun belt. "You'd best take your papa's Dragoon pistol. It's more powerful than that Confederate peashooter and twice as trustworthy. And take the shotgun as well. It may come in handy."

Joshua agreed. He buckled the belt around his narrow hips and felt the weight of the big revolver hang heavily against his right thigh. He recalled that he had always admired the Colt Dragoon; nickel plated with fancy scrolled engraving on the cylinder and barrel, and grips of polished ivory. He also recalled that it had a kick like a Missouri mule. But, then, he hadn't shot the thing since he was twelve years of age.

The old man slipped the thong with the wooden cross from around his neck. "Take this as well. It may be your only chance between life and death."

Joshua nodded, donned the necklace, and tucked it in his shirt collar. "I'll be leaving now," he said, tucking the Belgium scattergun beneath his arm.

"Could you do me one last favor?"

Joshua agreed that he would.

"Find my brother, Clarence, in the next town over and tell him to bring his horse and wagon, and come get me. I don't cotton to spending one more night alone in this place, even if the threat of evil is no longer here."

"I understand. I'll certainly do that."

George reached out and Joshua took his hand firmly. "I'll be praying for you in your travels, Mister Josh. And for the treacherous work you've got ahead of you."

"Much obliged," nodded the man in the black broadcloth suit. Then he turned and left the plantation house.

A few moments passed. With some effort, the old man left his chair before the hearth and made his way to one of the ballroom windows. He stood and watched through the broken panes as the tall Southerner slid the double-barreled shotgun into a leather scabbard buckled to the saddle. Then he slipped his right boot into the stirrup and swung atop the black horse. The rider regarded the ruins of the mansion one final time, then reined his mount toward the main road.

George sighed deeply and dabbed at his moist eyes with the sleeve of his woolen shirt. A heavy sorrow settled in his chest as he turned from the window and hobbled back to his place before the marble fireplace. For, deep down in his heart, he knew that it was the last time he would ever see the man named Joshua Wingade alive.

CHAPTER THREE

Cartersville, Georgia
Late September 1866

For two days, Joshua rode northward.

He was no scout or tracker like some men he had encountered during the War, but he had no need to be. The path of death and destruction Holland and his followers blazed across the Georgia landscape was apparent and unmistakable.

He found horses slaughtered by the side of the trail and their riders either missing or hung from the bows of trees. At one homestead, a man and woman had been impaled with fence posts and left there to perish in agony. Their faces, frozen in a rictus of pain and great loss, were turned skyward, as though begging God for mercy or demanding to know why He had allowed such a senseless demise to take place. Joshua considered burying the two, but he could figure no way to remove them and could find no axe in which to chop the posts down, so he left them where they were. It was a sorrowful thing to surrender them to the buzzards and ants, with no proper burial to conceal them.

Before he left, Joshua discovered the charred wood of a campfire and makeshift spit beneath a hickory tree near the cabin. Small, scorched bones littered the ground, with scarcely a bit of meat upon them. They were not those of an animal.

Further on, Joshua came upon a town. It had been burned to the ground. Only jagged pinnacles of charred timber stood where walls and jousts had once been. The earth of the street was stained dark with pools of congealed blood, but he discovered no victims. His black horse grew skittish, snorting and tossing its head. Joshua looked off toward a shadowy stretch of forest and, even though it was the noon of the day, he shivered, wondering what was concealed there until twilight.

At evening of the second day, as he approached the town of Cartersville, Joshua came upon another farmstead.

This one seemed deserted. There was not a person to be found. He looked for signs of death and destruction, like the other places, but there were none.

The farm was a small one; a single-story house, a barn, chicken coop, and a shed for curing meat. A swing made of a plank and two ropes hung from the bough of an oak in the yard, indicating that there had been children there.

He noticed that the front door of the structure stood open.

"Hello the house!" he yelled out. Joshua knew you could get yourself shot if you didn't let folks know you were coming. But the precaution was useless. No one answered.

He swung off the Morgan and tied the reins to the front porch railing. He mounted the low steps of the porch and warily peered inside. There was a single room beyond the doorway...a family room. A stone hearth, long eating table with four chairs, a sideboard, and an iron cook stove vented through the ceiling to the roof outside.

There was food on the table that had probably been there for a day or so. Green flies buzzed and covered fatback and beans, collard greens, and cornbread. Two of the chairs lay on the floor, overturned.

He checked the adjoining rooms...both bedrooms. No one. In a room bearing a large brass-framed bed, there was a cradle. It was empty. Inside laid a pale blue blanket with three drops of blood on the material.

Quietly, he walked back into the main room. The western windows gleamed crimson with the waning light of sunset. He knew that it would not be long before darkness began to descend.

Joshua was debating whether to spend the night in the empty house or ride further down the trail and camp somewhere else, when he heard a sound. A sound coming up through the cracks of the floorboards beneath his feet.

Someone was snoring.

Joshua's heart quickened. The first thing that came to mind was Elizabeth sleeping in that hollowed-out place in the cellar floor.

He looked toward the windows. The crimson had muted to a dark purple.

Quickly, he made his way across the floor and back onto the porch.

The horse's nostrils were flared. His hooves milled restlessly in the dust of the yard.

Joshua ran a trembling hand down the length of the animal's neck. "I know, boy," he said soothingly. "We're going."

He slipped the reins from the rail, swung into the saddle, and urged the horse away from the house. The shadows across the yard were longer and deeper than when he had first arrived and a growing chill hung in the air.

He was fifty yards from the house when a shrill noise cut through his ears.

The sound of nails pulling loose as floorboards were pried upward.

Joshua dug his boot heels into the flanks of the horse and left the farmstead at a gallop.

Half a mile down the road, he tugged the reins and slowed to a canter. He looked over his shoulder, but could see nothing. Gloom gathering amid the trees and darkened the ruts of the road.

Joshua lifted his eyes to the sky. Dark blueness grew deeper by the minute. He reined the horse to a halt and listened intently...perhaps for the flutter of wings. He recalled the bat in the cellar and knew that distance would be no obstacle to the things that had lain beneath the farmhouse floor.

He had traveled a quarter mile further when something made him stop again. For a moment, silence pressed against his ears. Then a sound echoed from nearby. One that turned the blood in his veins as cold as ice.

It was the giggling of a small child.

He looked off into the woods to his left. He saw nothing, just trees and dense underbrush. Against his better judgement, Joshua dismounted and drew his pistol.

What if it's a child from the farm? he wondered. *What if it escaped what happened to its folks and is lost in the woods?* He stepped off the dirt roadway and started through high weeds, toward a lightning-struck chestnut tree that stood several yards away.

But, if that were the case, it would be crying, wouldn't it? Not laughing.

He reached the tree. It was dead, its trunk split halfway by a bolt of heavenly fury. The giggle came again...magnified by the hollow of the tree.

Joshua hooked the toe of a boot in a crevice and lifted himself to look down into the dark opening. He could see nothing. The giggling stopped. He sensed tiny eyes staring up at him...studying him.

Still holding the Dragoon in his right hand, he dipped his other into his britches pocket and withdrew the tin of matches. Awkwardly, he fumbled it open, withdrew one, and returned the container to his pocket. Joshua took a deep breath and then struck the sulfur tip against the bark of the tree. It flared into life; first illuminating his face, followed by the contents of the hollow tree as he leaned forward and held it above the opening.

"Good God Almighty!" he whispered. His nerve threatened to leave him, but he held firm to it, allowing time for his mind to comprehend was he was gazing upon.

It was a baby, not even a year in age. If it had been alive, it would have been cute...precious. One that you would have wanted to cradle and cuddle. But it wasn't, and that made it a thing to fear and loathe. Its round, chubby-cheeked face was as pale as that of a china doll and its glistening eyes were completely black, as though the pupils had expanded and swallowed the whites whole. They twinkled keenly as a tiny, blue tongue ran hungrily across equally blue lips.

Slowly, it began to work its way upward, bracing its stubby arms and legs against the walls of the tree's inner hollow. The thing's belly gurgled and, eagerly, it cooed. It no longer craved mother's milk, but sustenance of a more sanguinary nature.

When it was almost to the opening in the trunk, its mouth grew wide, impossibly wide, as though its lower jaw had popped loose from its moorings and come unhinged. Bloodless gums began to sprout tiny fangs as sharp and jagged as sewing needles.

"Lord, please, forgive me," moaned Joshua. He lowered the Dragoon and pressed its muzzle against the baby's forehead. He had no doubt in his mind that the child's pale flesh was every bit as cold as the steel of the gun he held in his hand.

He thumbed back the hammer and squeezed the trigger. The 44-caliber pistol discharged, booming like a cannon in his ears. The darkness of the empty tree swallowed the tiny fiend, and he saw it no more. As the gun's report faded, Joshua listened, hoping...praying...that the thing was dead. A playful giggle told him it was not. The damage the lead projectile had wrought was bound to have been devastating, yet it lived. Or, rather, existed.

Joshua jumped down from the tree and stood in indecision for a long moment. Then he turned and walked back to his horse. Behind him, he could hear small sounds from the dark cradle of the burnt-out tree. An owl hooted somewhere off in the forest. The nocturnal sound elicited another giggle from the hidden thing. It was no longer afraid of things in the dark as it once had been. Now it was comfortable with night and its many playthings.

Leaving that horrid place, Joshua Wingade rode in darkness for several hours, putting many miles between him and the farmstead. When he finally rested for the night, his thoughts turned to the things beneath the floor, as well as the one that dwelt in the hollow tree, and he tossed and turned upon his blankets, and failed to sleep peacefully...if he slept any at all.

CHAPTER FOUR

Chattanooga, Tennessee
Early October 1866

Autumn grew cooler and more vibrant with leaves the color of fire as one month bled into the next. Joshua Wingade continued to ride northwestward, following the path of destruction Jules Holland and his outlaw gang had left in their wake.

Joshua rode through the town of Chickamauga, then grimly crossed the cannon-scarred fields where Rosecrans' Union Army of the Cumberland had clashed violently with Bragg's Confederate Army of Tennessee. During the three-day hell that had raged there, nearly forty thousand men had been wounded, captured, or killed. In Cherokee, Chickamauga meant "river of death", which was horribly accurate and prophetic, even though the largest body of water was no more than a small creek that wound through the pastures and forests to the north. The place was silent and solemn, and Joshua found himself urging his horse onward at a galloping pace, if only to pass that distressing place and leave its dark and violent history behind.

It wasn't long before he approached the lofty peaks of Lookout Mountain and entered the outskirts of Chattanooga. Hungry and weary, Joshua left the Morgan at a livery stable for some much needed rest and a trough of barley and oats. Then, slinging his saddlebags over his narrow shoulder, he crossed the street to a saloon, anxious for a meal and a shot or two of bourbon whiskey.

As he sat by the front window eating a dinner of steak, potatoes, and beans, the man noticed a cluster of women on the boardwalk outside. They were discussing a matter of great importance, their faces etched with concern and, yes, even fear. One out of the group was more adamant than the others; a short, buxom, middle-aged woman wearing a blue calico dress and white bonnet. The others seemed intent on stopping her from some grave errand she had taken upon herself, but she pulled away from their grasp and marched boldly to the door of the tavern. As Joshua poured more liquor from the bottle, he watched as the woman stepped inside, drawing the startled gaze of several men at the long mahogany bar. Then, surprisingly, she turned her eyes on him and walked over. Without hesitation, she pulled out the chair opposite him and sat down.

She regarded him sourly. "Sir, do you always dine wearing your hat?" she asked in distaste. Apparently, his lack of manners were not to her liking.

Joshua slowly chewed his steak and took another sip from his glass. "And do you have a habit of entering drinking establishments and conversing with strange men?" he wanted to know in return. "If you have a mind to proposition me, sorry, but I ain't interested."

The woman's broad face reddened as she realized he had practically called her a whore. "I'll have you know I'm a well-respected lady in this town. One of high-standing and influence. My name is Louisa Bradley and my husband is the marshal of this town."

"Comforting to know," Joshua said indifferently. "Now, if you'll allow me to eat in peace." He turned his eyes back to his plate. As he lifted his fork to his mouth, his hand trembled.

"Do you suffer from an aliment?" she asked tactlessly, making no move to leave her chair. "A palsy?"

Joshua frowned in embarrassment, returning the utensil to the china plate that held the remnants of his meal. There was something about the woman that grated on his nerves. "I don't believe that's any concern of yours, lady. Now, if you will move on..."

"I must warn you, sir... I am one known for speaking her mind," she declared. "I'll not budge from this spot until I've had my say!"

The tall Georgian sighed and sat back in his chair. "Very well then. What is on your mind and precisely how does it involve me?"

"Are you traveling northward after leaving here?"

"I am," he admitted.

"Then I seek a favor of you." Louisa took several gold coins from her handbag and laid them on the tabletop before him. "And am willing to pay generously for it."

Joshua ignored the money. "What is it that you want?"

"Three days ago, my husband, Elmer Bradley, and six deputized men left here in pursuit of a man named Holland and the rabble that accompanied him. There was a woman in their company as well." She lowered her voice. "A light-skinned colored girl. One with a veil upon her head and a dress of black taffeta and lace. The men rode horses...ornery critters that would just as soon take a bite out of you for no good reason...not gentle like most mounts. The woman drove a wagon of the type gypsies travel in, with a cabin rather than an open bed. It was also painted black and drawn by two coal-colored mares with marks upon their foreheads. White marks that resembled the crucifix of Christ...only upside down."

Joshua's stomach sank and he pushed his plate away, his appetite having faded. "Was there a young'un with them?" he asked. "A boy?"

Louisa Bradley considered the question. "Come to think of it, some did claim they heard the cries of a child inside the cabin, out of sight."

The tall man nodded. At least now he knew his pursuit was justified and that his son, Daniel, still lived. "Exactly what did this Holland do that caused your husband to gather a posse and go after him?"

The boldness in the woman's eyes faltered and fear surfaced. "He...he *defiled* my daughter, Bessie. Set upon her as she crossed the rear yard of our home in the middle of night, on her way to the privy."

Joshua chose his words carefully. "He took *advantage* of her?"

The matronly woman shook her head. "No...not in that way. He...he... God, please fortify me... He *bit* her and suckled at her throat. I know that is difficult to believe, but..."

Joshua's eyes softened and he lifted a gaunt hand. "Not as difficult as you might think. How old is your daughter?

"She is but fourteen years of age. My poor, little girl!"

He hesitated to ask, but knew that he must. "And where is she now?"

"In the cellar of the house," the woman said. Tears began to well in her eyes and, suddenly, her presence didn't annoy Joshua so greatly. "She hides down there during the daylight hours and sleeps. When the sun sets, she awakens and...and...oh, sir, it is much too awful to put into words!"

"She hunts," he said for her.

"Yes!" Louisa took a handkerchief from her bag and dabbed at her eyes. "So far it has only been for small things. The neighbor's yellow tabby...mice and toads in the garden beside the house. But I fear she will not be satisfied with such trivial...*sustenance.*" The woman shuddered at the thought. "Not much longer."

"So, your husband and his deputies went after them?"

"Yes, but we have heard nothing of them since," she said, her voice fearful and heavy with desperation. "I took the liberty of wiring the telegraph office in the town of Soddy-Daisy, twenty miles northeast of here, but they have seen no sign of Elmer or the others. I fear they have met disaster."

Joshua stared at the anxious woman. "And what is that you wish me to do?"

"As you ride, look for them," she implored. "When you reach town, or even beyond, wire me and tell me what you have found...or what you haven't. My husband is a brash and humorless man, but I adore him. And I fear for his life, as my acquaintances fear for the lives of their own men."

"Don't you have men here who will search for them?"

Louisa glared at the hunched backs of the men at the bar. "Men? Ha! There are none here at all! Only cowards!"

One of the men, a tall, broad-shouldered man with a graying beard, gathered the nerve to confront her. "Come now, Mrs. Louisa! What man in his right mind would go after them and chance crossing that ornery bunch? Remember what happened to Willie Stanton in this very saloon? How Holland's hired gun, that fella named Snake took offense to something Willie said? His gun had scarcely cleared leather before poor Willie had lost his nose and both ears to the shots he fired. Then that other one, the big'un called Hog, walked over with that Bowie of his and cleaved Willie's head from his neckbone with one swing of his arm."

A chubby, red-faced man next to the other nodded and downed half a mug of beer with one swallow. "And that deformed little bastard...the one called Rooster...laughing his damn, fool head off the whole time!"

"I recall," allowed the woman, "although I didn't see it for myself. But I will say that I'd grow a backbone and do something about it if someone had done such a thing to a good friend of mine!"

Ashamed, the two turned away from her and called for more liquor. The bartender—a squirrely little man with thick spectacles and his hair parted in the middle—stepped forward and replenished their waning glasses with fresh libations.

Joshua looked down at the gold on the table and pushed the coins back toward her. "I'd say I'm no braver than they are, but I'll do as you ask. I'll send word and let you know what I've seen...or if I haven't found them at all."

Louisa Bradley seemed appeased and satisfied. "That is all I ask. This awful uncertainty has me vexed...as well as what has become of our beloved Bessie." She extended her hand. "I'm appreciative of your kindness, Mister...?"

"Wingade," he answered, taking her fingers lightly. "Joshua Wingade of Athens."

She nodded and turned to leave. "Then I'll leave you to your meal and your travels."

As she started toward the saloon door, Joshua spoke. "Mrs. Bradley...you do know what your daughter has become, don't you?"

When Louisa turned around, her face was blanched and as pale as baking flour. "Yes... I fear that I do."

"Then you know what must be done."

Even during war, he had never seen such despair and sorrow as that which haunted the woman's tearful eyes. "I know," she admitted. "But...but I can't." She shook her head sadly, as though her child was already dead and buried, and not hiding in a cellar, sheltered from the rays of the sun. "I simply *can't!*"

After she had departed, Joshua sat there alone and silent. His plate sat before him, its contents growing cold, for what little appetite he had possessed was now completely gone. He contemplated Marshal Bradley and his posse, Louisa and her poor, doomed daughter...as well as the weeping of an unseen child concealed from sight in the back of a traveling wagon driven by a dark women in crow black raiment and lace.

Joshua had ridden a day and half, having found no sign whatsoever of those Louisa Bradley had wished him to keep vigilance for. He had seen other things, though...things that perplexed the mind and caused him to wonder just what manner of evil he was foolishly pursuing.

Near a white-washed church house on the outskirts of the settlement of Red Bank, he found a man standing in the grass near the side of the road. His hand was outstretched—accusingly—as though he were engaged in a fearful sermon. His other hand clutched a worn and dog-eared Bible. It had rained earlier that morning and the preacher stood, soaking wet, his face full of anger and defiance. It seemed he had been there for hours or perhaps even a day or so.

When Joshua dismounted to see to him, he found the man as rigid as a statue. His skin was as white as chalk and his hair like bailing wire. The Georgian could imagine the man casting scathing words of fire and brimstone at Holland and his travelers while they laughed and cursed his insolence. He reached out and touched the man's face and the cheek and a portion of the lower jaw crumbled away and fell at his feet. The Morgan walked forward, bent its head, and licked at the substance. Joshua suddenly saw it for what it was.

Salt.

How had they managed to turn the man of God into a hardened likeness akin to Lot's wife, who had been warned by angels and changed in an identical way as she gazed upon the chaotic fury of

Sodom and Gomorrah? For some odd reason, he felt the woman in black had something to do with the pastor's frightening transfiguration.

Joshua had also found a peculiar occurrence awaiting him in the town of Soddy-Daisy, the town Louisa had mentioned during their discussion in the saloon.

The doors of the shops and houses along the main thoroughfare were securely locked and the shutters closed and bolted tightly. He wondered what had happened there that had driven the residents to conceal themselves. As he reached a large oak in front of the courthouse at the far end of town, he knew. Four townsfolk had been strung up from the sturdy limbs by the ankles with heavy rope, the crowns of their heads barely a foot from the blood-soaked earth.

He couldn't tell whether they had been men or women, for they were only gory bones and nothing more. Although his mind railed against the thought, Joshua knew they had been skinned and gutted like deer, perhaps while they still lived. What had happened to their muscle, sinew, and organs was a mystery. But the man on the black roan could imagine the awful depravity that might have beset them.

He recalled the farm with the spit and fire, and the tiny, scorched bones underneath, gnawed and stripped of every last bit of meat.

It was at noon of the second day when Joshua Wingade knew that he had found what he had been searching for.

The black horse sensed it first. Its nostrils flared, and it halted in mid-stride. It blew nervously, and Joshua had to pull firmly on the reins to manage the steed. "What is it, boy? What spooks you so?"

Then he saw them up ahead. At first, from a distance, they appeared to be seven large, pale boulders scattered upon the road. But as he urged the horse nearer, he saw they were not mounds of stone at all. Nervously, he tied the animal to a sassafras tree and approached on foot.

The bundles were wrapped in a strange, bluish material much like the silk of the caterpillar nests that could be found in the boughs of trees in the South during the spring of the year. He returned to his horse and took a shaving razor from a pouch of his saddlebags. Kneeling before the first cocoon, he parted the tough threads with the honed edge.

It was a horse. A bay mare of chestnut brown that had been a fine piece of horseflesh at one time. Now it was dry and sunken, its fluids having been sucked and siphoned away. Joshua had no idea what had caused the animal's death, but whatever it was, it had been huge. He could tell by the two massive puncture wounds on the side of the horses neck, a good ten inches in length and six inches in depth.

The mount's saddle had been chewed and sharply scored, and was coated with congealed blood. He knew if he opened the other silken pods, he would find other horses in similar states of desecration.

He walked back to the Morgan and pulled the twelve-gauge from its sheath, then gathered a handful of brass shells from the saddlebags and deposited them in the side pocket of his frock coat. He looked around, searching for some sign of the riders; the Chattanooga lawman and his posse. At first, he saw nothing. Then something caught his eye.

Amid a stand of long-leaf pine trees a hundred yards away, a grayish-blue mist seemed to have settled. But he knew it was no fog. The morning was sunny and the weather clear.

Joshua hesitated. A deep feeling of dread settled within him, and he knew that what awaited within the timber was something he would not want to lay witness to. He considered returning to his horse and leaving right then and there. But he recalled Louisa Bradley's tearful face, already mourning over loved ones who still lived, but were lost, and he knew he had no choice but to hold true to his promise.

Gripping the Belgian scattergun tightly in both hands, he departed the roadway and waded through dense thicket to the stand of pines.

The nearer he drew to the mist between the trees, the more he realized it was not what it appeared to be, but what he feared it to be.

He stepped into a small clearing amid the pines. Joshua could only stand and stare for a long moment, forcing his mind to accept what his eyes were attempting to comprehend. He had seen nothing like it in his thirty-two years and hoped to never see anything like it ever again.

Stretched between two trees was a heavy mat of silk, secured from various branches and limbs. It resembled a massive cobweb, like the ones he had grown up seeing amid the rhododendrons and lilies of his mother's flower garden. Except that this one held no flies or small insects entangled in its strands.

Trapped within the web were the bodies of seven men. Or what had once been men. Their bodies were twisted; the arms and legs disjointed and at odds with one another. The flesh of their faces and hands were pale gray and shriveled, sapped of the color of life and clinging tightly to bone, as though the muscle underneath had dissolved and wasted away. Their clothing hung loosely on their frames, for any brawn or fat had also been stolen from them. They resembled garish scarecrows more than anything else, and there was a smell about them, like old books in a library or the dust of things long left abandoned in an attic.

Joshua's eyes settled on one that hung directly in the center of the web. He seemed no different than the others, still and emaciated, except for one thing. A brass star pinned to the breast of his vest. Engraved in the metal were the words U.S. MARSHAL.

"Elmer Bradley," he said softly.

Abruptly, the body lurched violently and the head—no more than an eyeless skull—lifted, causing the dry flesh to split and reveal stark, white bone across the forehead and cheeks.

"Yes?" The man's voice was hollow, like wind whistling through bone robbed of its marrow. "Who is there?"

Joshua stumbled backward. He turned away and breathed deeply, attempting to steady himself. When he turned back, he regarded the marshal with pity.

"What happened here? What did this to you?"

Elmer Bradley spoke haltingly. Something in his throat was dried up and broken and it rattled as he talked. "Mymahthu," he said, his mummified face crackling in a rictus of pure terror. "It said its name...was Mymahthu. It wanted us to know...who it was that feasted upon us."

"How did it come to be here?" Joshua asked him. "Did it have anything to do with Jules Holland?"

"No, not him. But...the witch..."

"The negro woman? The one dressed in black?"

The thing that had been Elmer Bradley coughed violently. Teeth, cracked and yellow, dislodged from his dry gums and fell at Joshua's feet. "Yes! She...she was the one...who brought it about!" The lawman frowned, as though attempting to assemble his thoughts. "We rode around a bend in the road and there she was...just standing there...alone. No sign of Holland or the other three. She had a book in her hand...an old book. Bound in leather...but not cowhide. It was of no animal hide at all. There were things about that leather binding....moles and scars...freckles...the shriveled nipple of a woman's teat. It was...*unholy*!"

"What did she do then?" Joshua knew he must ask his questions swiftly, for Elmer Bradley was beginning to disintegrate before his very eyes. The lawman's left ear broke off from the side of his head and tumbled down his shoulder and collarbone. It caught, upside down, on one of the points of the brass star.

"She stood there and openly read from the book," Bradley told him. "It was of a language foreign to me...a tongue of darkness and evil. She began to move her hand in circles...small at first, then larger and larger as her voice began to rise.

An odor filled the air…like in a blacksmith's shop…hot, like sparks from a mallet against a horseshoe. I was sitting atop my horse, looking at that damned book when she reached the end of her…chanting. The cover of skin rippled with gooseflesh, like someone who was chilled to the bone in winter. Then…oh, Lord and Savior help us…it happened!"

"What?" urged Joshua. The flesh of the marshal's right hand turned to dust and slipped away, revealing stark, naked bone. "What happened then?"

"There was… There was a…*hole*. A hole out of nowhere. It opened up, hanging there in the air. It began the size of a keyhole…then grew bigger and bigger. Outside the hole, you could see the sky above…the earth of the road…and the woods on either side. But, inside…there was darkness…and other things. Swirls of light…stars, akin to those in the sky…but like none I've ever laid eyes on before." An expression of absolute horror seized the man's visage and Joshua was afraid his jaw would completely unhinge and fall away. "Then…then there it was! Crawling out of that hole in the air…stinking of death and destruction…a dreadful sight to behold!"

Joshua considered asking him what the thing had been or how it had looked…but he didn't. The emaciated man shuddered and shook so forcefully, that he was afraid he would crumble to pieces if pressed too hard. Besides, just looking at the way the men had been trussed up and mercilessly fed upon gave Joshua a fair idea of what manner of creature they had encountered.

"We unloaded all we had into it, but it merely laughed and kept on coming. I've encountered horrible things in my time as a law officer…men who raped children…husbands who murdered their wives and young'uns without regret…but I've never known evil like the thing that came out of that hole." Joshua could tell by the expression on the man's face that he would have wept in terror if only he possessed eyes to do so with. "Mymahthu! That was the name it proclaimed…prideful and vindictively…like a god before maggots. It spoke in the tongue the witch had read from that damnable book…but it came from inside our heads…not through our ears. And we understood. Lord help us…we understood ever word!"

"What took place then?"

"It overtook us…swept us off our horses with those hairy arms it had. Must have been ten or twelve of them. It…it had a tail, too. Like a scorpion's. Speared us with the tip and poisoned us…paralyzed us. Hauled us, limp as rag dolls into the woods and built this contraption I hang in now. Then it returned to the road and fed upon the horses. We could do nothing but dangle here and listen to those animals scream. Then it came back and took care of us, one by one."

"What happened to it afterwards?" Joshua wanted to know. "Where did it go?" He looked off into the dark forest beyond the pine grove and shuddered.

"I can't rightly say." Another fit of violent coughing, causing the man to swing back and forth in the monstrous web. Joshua could hear the man's ribs snapping and splintering within the cage of his sunken chest. "I reckon I blacked out. Maybe it went back into that hole in the air…back to the hell from where it came."

Joshua Wingade stood there for a long moment, regarding the lawman grimly. "There's nothing I can do for you, is there?"

"No," said Bradley. "But I it won't be much longer… I can feel it. The others died hours ago." His mouth twisted into a hideous grin that was more tragedy than humor. "When it came to giving up, I always was a stubborn son of a bitch."

"Your wife came to me, concerned about your whereabouts. I promised I would wire her and let her know what became of you."

"No!" protested Bradley with his last ounce of strength. "Please…don't. I'd rather she never know what happened to us than come looking for us and find us like this. And she would, too. She's an exasperating and tiresome woman at times, but I love her dearly. She would rent a horse from the livery and set out to find me. And, if she did, would that thing…that Mymahthu…be here to meet her? No…leave it be. Let me die knowing that she is safe at home and not wandering through this territory, at risk of being attacked by that monstrosity."

Safe at home, thought Joshua. He thought of the Bradleys' young daughter and wondered if that were possible while the girl roamed the dark of night, hungering for more than cats and small critters.

"Tell me something," said Joshua, sensing the end was near. "Did you see a child? A boy about eight years of age?"

"No," Bradley told him. "I saw no one at all. No one but that black bitch with that damnable book of hers." The marshal's head sagged and his ravaged face turned in the Georgian's direction. "May I ask what your name is?"

"Joshua," he told him and left it at that.

"I'm glad you found me. It ain't right for a man to die alone. Particularly a death such as this."

Before Joshua could answer in reply, the end came. Elmer Bradley's mouth stretched wide and a horrid sound rattled from his chest. A low, hollow moan that rose from the bone-dry channel of his gullet and, gaining momentum and volume, erupted from his open mouth with a spray of dust and fury. At the same instant, the marshal's body seemed to implode. The chest and abdomen, the eyeless face and the skull it belonged to, crumpled and sank, as though the final remnants of mind and body had been completely exhausted. Joshua watched in horror as Bradley began to dissolve before his eyes. His skin, gray and sapped of moisture, flaked away and was carried away by a northern breeze, leaving only bones dangling within the silky strands of Mymahthu's web.

Stunned, Joshua Wingade turned and made his way back to his horse. The Morgan no longer seemed disturbed, for the things suspended between the trees were only things now...inanimate and lifeless.

As he swung back into the saddle, Joshua felt strangely uneasy. Other than the horse beneath him, he was alone... Or was he? After Marshal Bradley and his posse had been abducted and fed upon, had the portal of the black witch reopened?

Had this monster...this Mymahthu...returned to its realm...the hole conjured from out of nowhere? Or was it still here, hidden and satisfied for the present, somewhere in the dark forest?

As Joshua Wingade rode away, he could almost imagine it was staring after him from the shadows of boughs and branches, with a thousand dark and otherworldly eyes.

CHAPTER FIVE

A Backwoods Clearing near McMinnville, Tennessee
October 1866

Joshua built a fire in the center of a small clearing, a mile or so past
the town of McMinnville. He stoked it with fallen branches and bits
of dead brush, coaxing the flames hotter and higher than he was
normally accustomed to. The October night was particularly chilly.
He expected a hard frost to whiten the ground come morning, as well
as his blanket and the crown of his hat. If additional warmth from the
fire could alleviate his awakening to such bone-chilling misery at the
first light of dawn, then the extra effort of gathering fodder for the
blaze would be well worth it.

He ate a cold supper of jerky and a napkin full of cornbread he
had liberated from his last sit-down meal back in Chattanooga. He
practically had no appetite at all, but knew sustenance was essential
to keep his strength up and his fortitude stable and on course. It had
been two days since his unpleasant encounter with the ambushed
posse and their head-strong leader, and it still haunted him greatly.

Until that discovery, his motivation had been simple. Track the culprits and save his boy…then return home and continue life in Georgia without Elizabeth. To simply survive the trying ordeal and attempt to build a future beyond what had taken place at the plantation during his absence.

But those hopes and the reality of actually accomplishing what he had originally set out to do seemed almost unattainable now. He considered all that he had seen, all that he had lain witness to, since his return home to Athens several weeks ago. The occurrences and atrocities perpetrated by the one called Jules Holland and his band of dark accomplices.

Disturbed, he stared into the flames and considered them, one by one.

Elizabeth in the cellar.

The two impaled upon posts and a scattering of tiny bones beside a mealtime fire.

The things sleeping beneath the boards of the floor.

The baby in the tree.

The preacher of salt.

The butchered four that hung from the oak.

The silken tombs of the exsanguinated horses.

And, lastly, the web of Mymahthu and its entangled prey.

You're insane, he told himself. *You're aiming to go up against these…these fiends…the way you are now?* He lifted his hands before his eyes. They shuddered fiercely in the flickering glow of the fire. *And alone? One man against four…and not knowing if they are even men at all? And the woman who can cast spells and conjure monsters out of thin air?*

Joshua almost packed up his gear at that very moment with the intention of heading back to Georgia the following morning. He almost abandoned the hopeless quest he had set upon…figuring to cut his losses and accept the terrible misfortune that had been dealt him. But a single consideration prevented him from doing so.

Daniel.

It had been five years since he had laid eyes on the boy, but that had never decreased his affection for him. Daniel had been four years old at the beginning of the War; he was scarcely nine now. Joshua had only received three letters from Elizabeth during the duration of the conflict. One had included a tintype photograph of her and the boy at the age of six. He had resembled his father; tall, gangly, with hair as dark as a raven. In her letter, his wife had said the child's demeanor was similar to Joshua's as well. Moody and often melancholy...and doggedly resolute when it came to accomplishing an objective or getting his way.

Does he even know me? Joshua wondered. To even consider such a thing was disheartening. *Would he even recognize me if he laid eyes on me?*

Still, that failed to matter. Someone had invaded his home and destroyed his family. They had turned his beloved into a hellion not of this world and abducted his only son. To abandon Daniel now...to leave him in the clutches of the wicked for only God knew what reason...that would be unforgiveable.

He took the Colt revolver from its holster. It was large and cumbersome and trembled in his faltering grasp. The Dragoon was a powerful piece of gunmetal, but, alone, it was ineffective and useless. It was the man behind the gun that gave it its threat...the precision of the shooter's eye and the steadiness of his hand. The War Between the States had robbed Joshua Wingade of both; had left him a broken man whose sense of self-worth and confidence was shattered, and inflicted him with a deep-seeded fear and loathing of firearms. Or, more precisely, things that were instrumental in the wanton destruction and taking of human life.

Dejected, he returned the gun to its rightful place. The Georgian wondered if he would be able to use it, and use it effectively when the time came. And, when he used it, if it would even matter at all against men such as the ones he now pursued.

Joshua readied his bedroll near a deadfall, then settled in for the night. The evening was brisk and his woolen blanket did little to insulate him from the declining temperature. He retrieved a spare garment from his saddlebags, wadded it up, and made himself a makeshift pillow. He bundled it behind his head on the curve of the log, covered his face with his hat, and soon found himself drifting off, the fire popping and crackling several feet beyond his feet.

As exhaustion overtook him and he fell asleep; he recalled a similar October evening, but one that seemed to echo from countless years ago. He sat on a rug before a marble fireplace, his young son cradled in his lap. As he read Daniel a storybook—*The Gorilla Hunters: A Tale of the Wilds of Africa*—Elizabeth lounged in a chair nearby, indulging in her needlework by lamplight. He glanced up from his reading and smiled at her, and she smiled back; gently, lovingly, grateful for the time they shared. It was a precious moment...one of pleasantry and peace. A perfect, golden evening.

In his memory, Daniel had looked up at him, eyes bright and full of endearment. "I love you, Papa," he had said, snuggling warmly against his father's chest.

"I love you, too, son," he whispered into the frigid night.

Then slumber claimed him, deeply, and without mercy.

So...you have finally come.

At first, he thought the voice had come to him in a dream. It seemed to reverberate through his mind, rather than his ears. Then a mounting thrill of alarm gripped him and he pulled his hat away from his eyes.

A man stood across the campfire from him. He was unnaturally tall and gaunt, and was dressed in a long, black greatcoat and high-peaked hat of the same dark hue. His face was as pale as candle tallow and his hair was as colorless as a winter's snow.

A peculiar expression possessed his lean face—a mixture of amusement and contempt. "What a dreadful disappointment," uttered the man, his voice heavy with a distinctive European accent. "That my adversary—the one who has pursued me so very far—would be a man as utterly unremarkable as this."

Joshua knew immediately who it was that faced him. He flung his blanket aside and fumbled for his sidearm. Soon, it was clear of its holster and its barrel leveled at the thing named Jules Holland. The gun jittered violently in his hand, causing the metal to rattle noisily.

"He suffers from a palsy," observed one of three men who stood behind Holland. The fellow was small, skinny, and physically deformed. Great, loose flaps of flaccid skin dangled like a fleshen beard beneath his chin and a larger, thicker one, mottled red in color, hung across his forehead, giving him the appearance of a human fowl. He wore the tattered remnants of a butternut uniform and the gray forage cap of the Confederacy. Around his narrow waist was a tanned belt bearing a holstered 42-caliber LeMat revolver and a calvary saber nestled in a long scabbard of hammered brass.

"That ain't it, Rooster," claimed the one next to him. "He's scared shitless."

Joshua's attention was shifted to the second man. He was of medium height, dressed in a coal black shirt and britches, and hand-stitched boots with jagged brass spurs affixed behind the heels. His low, black hat bore a band of equally brass studs shaped like tiny death-heads. He wore a brace of twin Remington revolvers, oiled and blued, with fancy Mother of Pearl handles. But it was his face and hands that unnerved the Georgian the most. For the diamond patterns of a timber rattler were etched across his forehead and cheeks, as well as down his wrists and fingers. Joshua had seen such men before; tattooed performers in traveling shows and carnivals during his travels through Virginia, Kentucky, and Tennessee. Except the patterns on this one looked to be genuine in nature, and not embellished from needle and ink. His eyes were yellow and the pupils narrow and vertical, rather than round like a normal man's. When he smiled, his teeth were curved and wretchedly sharp at the tips.

"You are wrong as well, Snake," said a third man. He was massive of height and girth, dressed in a long coat of tanned leather that resembled no animal hide Joshua had ever laid eyes on. His face was broad, portly, and swine-like in nature, and the teeth at the corners of his mouth jutted from the cradle of his lower jaw, thick and curved much like the tusks of a wild hog. "He is seized with anticipation...anxious for the kill...poised for the first shot!'

"No, Boar," Jules Holland told him. The vampire studied Wingade curiously. "His nerves...his very constitution...has been shattered beyond recovery. Not from terror or anxiety, but the very toll taken by war and its collective horrors."

"Your woman was the screaming vixen in Georgia, was she not?" asked Boar with a leer that swallowed his tiny eyes into slits. "An unwilling one, she was, but sufficient. She was our vessel to be filled...and she was...again and again."

Snake chuckled. "Ssssshe was sssssweet," he said softly. A narrow tongue—slick, gray, and forked at the tip—swept slowly across his jagged teeth. "Sssssso ssssweet."

I am at odds with the dregs of Hell, Joshua thought, his mind racing with alarm. *How will I possibly survive this? How will I get*

Daniel back? Appeal to their mercy? The way they stood and regarded him, like a squirming maggot upon cow shit, told him they were incapable of such.

"I... I am Joshua Wingade," he stammered. "I have come for my son."

"Yes," said Holland. He crouched and faced the Georgian. The dancing flames of the campfire illuminated the vampire's narrow face, revealing deeply-etched lines and eyes that had seen the passing of ages. "I know who you are and why you have come."

Joshua straightened up until he sat erect, his back resting against the cold, hard column of the fallen tree. He glared at the man, attempting to appear as menacing as he possibly could. "Then you know that I shall take him from you."

Jules Holland smiled. His strong, white teeth had altered themselves. The incisors were now longer and sharper, hanging an inch lower than the others. "You may try...but, so far, you are not doing a very adequate job of it."

"A piss poor job, I'd hazard to say!" snapped Rooster. He spat into the fire. His saliva popped and hissed as it was consumed.

"Why?" Joshua asked the stately man in the black coat and hat. "Why have you taken him?"

"Because I crave a progeny...a *successor*," Holland explained, as if to a simpleton. An expression crept into his icy blue eyes, or rather several combined. Sorrow. Regret. Longing. And perhaps even self-loathing. "The way I am...what I became many centuries ago...has robbed me of the ability to procreate. My seed is inanimate and cold. It has no purpose...no promise. It resides within me, wasted. I have claimed many brides...your delicate Elizabeth among them. They have brought me fleeting moments of sustenance and amusement...but they were never able to provide me with what I truly craved. A son."

"So, you figured to take mine." Joshua felt the heat of anger press pass his terror and despair. He cocked the Colt's hammer, cycling a load into place. He fought to control his nerves and managed to steady the big revolver long enough to aim squarely at the vampire's face.

"You must know that a bullet will not slay me," Holland said, shaking his head incredulously. "That it will only be a wasted effort. A squandering of powder and lead, and nothing more."

"Perhaps. But it shall bring a moment of satisfaction, at the very least."

Joshua squeezed the trigger. The Dragoon boomed with a burst of flame and a thick, gray cloud. The bullet struck Holland in the right side of the face, directly below his eye. The impact of the projectile tore away his cheekbone and a fragment of his upper lip. For an instant, he teetered on his heels and Joshua was certain he would fall forward into the fire. But then he smiled. It was a horrid thing to look upon. A gaping wound of torn, decayed tissue and ancient, shattered bone. The exposed fangs, set in pale and bloodless gums, grinned wickedly in triumph. Then, Holland's face mended itself. Bone knitted with bone, and flesh with flesh, until it was whole once again.

"Now," he said softly, almost regarded the tall man with pity. "What did that accomplish?" The vampire glanced over his shoulder. "Rooster…disarm this impotent wretch."

Startled, Joshua shifted his gun toward the skinny fellow in the Confederate cap. But the man was much too swift. Laughing, he leapt across the fire. His hand—wrinkled and yellow, like the talons of his namesake—grasped the handle of his sword. He withdrew it with a steely clash of metal against metal, and brought it down before the Southerner could withdraw. The curved blade of the saber cleaved Joshua's right arm away cleanly at the shoulder. As the appendage dropped into the autumn leaves, still clutching the Dragoon pistol, he witnessed his life's blood spurting into the night air, jetting hot and free from the containment it had known all his life.

"You will be dead within a quarter hour," Holland said grimly. "But I am not without a heart, even as frigid and inert as it is." He stood and called into the darkness beyond Snake and Boar. "Evangeline! Bring the boy!"

Even though wracked with agony, Joshua managed to peer past the four men. At the edge of the clearing was a black wagon drawn by two equally ebony horses. He watched as a woman appeared, dragging a sobbing, struggling child by one hand. When they reached the illumination of the campfire, Joshua studied the two. The boy was the one he regarded first. He was much older than the child in the tintype that rested in the inner pocket of his frock coat. Taller, thinner, his black hair shaggy and unkempt about his ears and the nape of his neck. His eyes, the same slate gray hue as his father's, were red and his face was dirty, distinctly etched with trails left by frightened and embittered tears.

Joshua turned his eyes from the boy to the one who held him. The woman named Evangeline was a negro, but her skin was light; the color of cream in black coffee. It was obvious that one of her parents, mother or father, had been Caucasian in race. Her hair was braided into tight strands that hung clear past her shapely shoulders and conjured images from Greek mythology; the serpentine locks of the evil Medusa.

The witch's eyes were not dark, but as green as a cat's and nearly as luminant in the glow of the fire. She was attired in a long dress of black taffeta, with clinging sleeves from shoulder to wrist, and a skirt that fell completely to the earth, draping upon the ground and obscuring her feet. A sheer, black veil that appeared to be more cobweb than lace descended from the crown of her head and swathed her countenance, but not to the point of obscurity. She wore a broach at her throat, but like none Joshua had ever seen. It seemed to be constructed of bone and etched with a five-pointed star enclosed within a circle. In the center of that symbol—one he knew to be the profane configuration of a pentagram—was the image of a goat-headed man with long, spiral horns. Set within the pits of the devil's eyes were tiny rubies that twinkled in the flames of the campfire.

"Allow him a parting moment with the child," Holland instructed.

The woman flung the child so violently that Joshua was certain he would lose his footing and fall into the fire. But the boy corrected himself and was soon on his knees in the leaves next to him.

"P-papa?" Daniel asked hesitantly. His eyes were a mixture of conflicting emotions; confusion, relief, sorrow, and horror. "Is it really you?"

"Yes, son," gasped Joshua. His head began to swim as weakness slowly overcame him. "It's been a long time."

The boy began to cry. "They...they killed Mama!" he moaned. He stared at the ragged stump. Its spurt had begun to slow, changing into a sluggish flow. "And they've...they've cut your arm away!"

"I came to deliver you boy, but I failed," apologized his father. "I'm sorry for that."

Daniel's face contorted into a wet mask of hopelessness and intense fear. It was as though he realized his final chance for salvation had been lost and had resigned himself to that awful fact. "I thank you just the same, Papa."

Joshua's eyesight began to falter and dim. The ache of the severed arm seemed dull and distant now. "I... I had to. I love you, son."

The child wailed and launched himself at the dying man. His arms entwined Joshua's neck and he clung tightly, defying Holland or Evangeline or even the Reaper himself to pull him away. He buried his face into his father's chest and wept bitterly. Joshua felt the boy's tears seep through his shirt and warmly dampen the flesh of his chest. It was a heartbreaking sensation...like a sorrowful and parting gift between family who would never see one another again.

"Take the boy," Holland said.

Evangeline skirted the fire and grasped the boy beneath the pits of his arm. He shrieked and sobbed as he was drawn away, back beyond the glow of the fire, into the night.

The vampire stood for a long moment and regarded the tall Georgian with disdain. "I have tired of this wretched worm" he said. "Do as you will and then end him. Afterward, we will be on our way."

The one named Boar walked over and glowered at the man slumped against the log. His eyes strayed to one of several patches of fungus that grew upon the deadfall. The plant glowed an eerie greenish-yellow in the darkness, despite the light of the fire. He dug a clump away with the jagged nail of his thumb and held it in front of Joshua's face. "Lookee here, you miserable bastard!" His breath was rank and sickening, and stank of rotten meat. "Foxfire. See how it glows of its own accord?"

Even as his strength faded, Joshua twisted his head to the side as Boar brought the luminant substance within an inch of his left eyeball.

"It is exquisite, don't you think? A lovely thing to behold. But it burns. It burns like the smoldering footstones of Hades. And it blinds!"

Without further hesitation, the human swine pressed the glowing fungus into the orb of Joshua Wingade's eye and ground it in. Despite his weakness, the man reacted violently, bucking wildly as the foxfire scalded his eye and robbed it of its ability to function. His screams rang shrilly throughout the October night, rising past the tops of the trees that bordered the clearing, piercing the heavens with its intensity. It was the forlorn cacophony of a spirit driven to imminent and irrevocable defeat...anguish, suffering, and remorse formed into an ugly, prolonged, keening wail.

"I'm finished with the gutless cur," growled Boar, abandoning the agonized man as though he had grown weary of the torment he had inflicted. "You may end him now, Snake."

The serpentine gunman stepped forward. The diamond patterns of his flesh expanded as his grin widened. "Ah, with pleasure, hermano. With pleasssssure."

Joshua stared up at the gunman with his one good eye and, in weak defiance, raised his one remaining hand as though to ward off the inevitable with fragile flesh and bone. "No...please...my son."

"Don't fret. He will be well taken care of," replied the thing in man's clothing. He shucked a single revolver from his gun belt and crisply cocked the hammer. His aim was unwavering as he centered his sights squarely between Joshua's eyebrows.

Somewhere his son cried out for him.

"Hush, child," said the voice of Evangeline. "Your father is dead."

But...but... I'm not...

A tragic range of emotions flash through a man's mind at the point of death.

Sorrow.

Regret.

Loss.

And, sometimes, unbridled rage...at the injustice of it all.

"Daniel!" his father screamed. "I will come for you! I promise!"

Snake laughed. "Save your breath for prayers. Savor this moment...for it shall be your last." He took a step closer, bringing the gun within a foot of the man's face. "Tell my brethren in Purgatory that I said 'howdy.' They will torment you well."

The muzzle of the Remington yawned like the mouth of an empty cavern. But Joshua knew that was a lie. Something awaited him within. Something small and quick and cast of bad intent and wanton waste.

When the time of annihilation came in explosive powder, flame, and lead, the man named Joshua Wingade neither saw it nor felt it.

He simply failed to be.

CHAPTER SIX

Site of a Killing near McMinnville, Tennessee
Mid-October 1866

"Am I in Heaven or Hell?"

"Neither. You're where you began and where you ended. Not exactly resurrection in the Christian sense of the word…but about as close as you can get, if you leave the Almighty out of it."

Joshua opened his one good eye.

The pale light of dawn met him, etching his surroundings in a stark pallet of assorted grays. He was sitting at the base of a hickory tree, his hat and mended frock coat on the ground beside him. He recognized the place. It was the clearing in the woods.

The place of his murder the night before.

Stiffly, he turned his head and looked at the one who had spoken.

The man was a negro, as black as pitch and as bald as a billiard ball. He was short and whipcord lean, and was dressed in traveling clothes that looked to be a rank stranger to the wash tub; a dingy white, collarless shirt, brown vest with all manner of pouches and pockets, woolen britches with faded, red suspenders, and mule-eared boots that looked to have trod a thousand miles or more. There was a dusty, gray bowler hat perched jauntily upon his hairless head. The sweat-stained crown was encircled with a band of tanned snake hide, copperhead from the pattern of the scales. An assortment of necklaces hung about the man's neck. They were charms and talismans from the looks of them; a chain of gator teeth, three tiny glass bottles of green, red, and blue on a silver chain, a leather thong bearing three bird feathers from an eagle, owl, and buzzard, and the dried and shriveled foot of a chicken.

He displayed an uneven picket of silver and gold teeth when he smiled. His demeanor seemed begrudgingly benevolent, with a dash of sassiness and sarcasm thrown into the pot for seasoning.

"So, how do you be feeling this glorious morning?" the man asked. He sat cross-legged before the campfire Joshua had built the evening before, pouring himself a cup of coffee that looked thick and strong enough to float a horseshoe and the mallet that made it.

"Oh, fine and dandy...considering I shouldn't be breathing at all."

The black man rolled his eyes and grinned. "Truthfully, you're not even doing that. Nor is your heart beating. You're just...let us say...present and accounted for."

"But the question is...*why*? I recall something...that happened afterward. Reaching out to shake the hand of Jesus...and, all of a sudden, I'm here again."

"Yes, Lord Jesus is like that. Loves you and me unconditionally if we follow the narrow path. But don't let the Messiah fool you. He's coming back someday...brandishing a golden sword and riding a white stallion, hellbent on kicking some heathen ass."

Joshua frowned. He found it difficult to do so. The muscles of his face seemed slack and unwilling to cooperate. "A mighty shitty thing to do, dragging a man away from his savior like that." He looked at the fellow. "And how, in tarnation, did you manage to do it? Bring me back, I mean."

The man mulled it over in his mind for a moment. "Does the term *zombie* ring a bell with you? If not, it's understandable. They're few and far between this far north. But back in Louisiana and the islands, they're tripping over one another, they're so plentiful."

"I've heard tell of it," Joshua admitted. "So, I'm sort of a walking dead man."

"Yes," admitted the man in the derby. "But one with a purpose."

"And what in Sam Hill would that be?"

"To fulfill your promise. To the boy."

His sluggish thoughts seemed to solidify then and he remembered the boy crying out for him. The gunslinger drawing and cocking his pistol. And Joshua's final vow.

I will come for you! I promise!

Joshua nodded grimly. "Yes, I see now."

"You do still have feelings for the boy, do you not? You still *love* him?"

If his heart had still pumped like a living man, it would have quickened in pace. But even though it hung, flaccid and cold within his chest, the emotion that seized him was genuine.

"Of course, I do."

"And you are faithful to the memory of your wife, is that right? For the horrid way they violated her…made her into what she had become… That deserves an extra measure of punishment, don't you think?"

"Yes. There's no denying it."

"Then we must go after Holland and his entourage," the black man insisted. "Liberate your son from his bondage and deliver lasting retribution upon their heads."

" *We?*" questioned the Georgian. "You're aiming to go with me?"

"I certainly am…if you think you can tolerate my company."

"I don't even know who you are."

"Well now, then allow me to introduce myself," the man said, rising to his feet. He swept his bowler hat from his head, nearly blinding Joshua with the shine of his scalp. "I am Job."

The dead man stared at him. "Job. Like that fella in the Bible that Satan tormented to no end?"

"Precisely! And like my namesake, I too have suffered my share of trials and tribulations."

Joshua grunted. "What happened? Was your master cruel to you?" He nodded to thick scars that peeked from beneath the man's shirt collar and the ends of his sleeves.

Job's precious metal grin faded and his features tensed. "I've never bowed to a master and never shall. I'd rather slit my own throat with a razor than be claimed as another man's property." He unbuttoned the cuff of one sleeve, showing off his forearm, over and under. Ugly, circular patterns branded his dark skin. "Wasn't what you thought, was it? No whip or strop has marred my flesh. Boils...like those endured by that woe begotten soul from the Land of Uz."

Joshua recalled the Bible stories his mother had told him when he was young. "Did a great wind drop a roof upon your children's heads and kills them?"

Job's countenance grew even more morose. "No sir, but it'd been better for me if they had. Each and every one has gone astray...some to worse mischief than the others. They might as well be dead and buried in their old pappy's eyes." His gaze centered on Wingade's pale, mustachioed face. "And your own flesh and blood will fall victim to vice and corruption—probably worse than any you could imagine—if we don't find him and deliver him from it soon."

Something about the little man bothered him. "What are those doodads hanging around your neck? Good luck charms?"

"Maybe to some. For others, they are misery and heartache," Job told him proudly. "They are the tools of my trade. Amulets and potions to cast a variety of cures and curses upon the well-deserved."

"So, you're a witch doctor?"

"Hell no! I'm a mojo man from the bayous of Bogalusa Parish in the swamps of Louisiana. Not that the church claims me as one of their own. They don't hold to the distasteful aspects of my specialty, so to speak."

The tall man didn't seem particularly pleased. "So, you did some conjuring to make me what I am? Voodoo or some such mumbo jumbo?"

"Don't be disrespecting it now!" Job said in protest. "It brought you back, didn't it?"

"Not sure if that's a blessing or a curse, to tell the truth." Joshua prodded at the bullet hole in his forehead. It had been plugged up with clay or some such material. Then he glanced down and suddenly realized his right arm was back in its rightful place. "What'd you do? Grow me a new one?"

Job laughed. "Now that'd be a trick I haven't mastered yet. I sewed it back on with catgut string and a little black magic. You know, I had to sacrifice my fiddle strings to mend your confounded appendage. I won't be able to play nary a square-dancing tune until we get to a general store the next town over."

The Georgian flexed his hand and found it in fair working order. "Who are you? Doctor Frankenstein?"

Job frowned sourly. "Who the hell would that be?"

"It was from a book I read once," Joshua told him. Steadying himself with the aid of the tree, he rose to his feet and donned his coat and hat. "Don't you read books? Or can you even read at all?"

"Oh, I can read me some books, but not the kind you'd dare lay a hand on," the negro proclaimed. "Ancient tomes that would make your frigging sawbones Frankenstein look like a dadgum fairy tale!"

The cadaver stretched his arm. "Feels *different*. Not like it was before I...died."

"Hold your hand out," suggested the mojo man. "Fingers straight, palm downward."

Joshua did as he requested. Both arm and hand were rock steady, with no tremor to them at all. "Well, I reckon death cured my case of bad nerves."

"Ain't got no nerves to you at all now," Job explained. "The dead can't feel pain, can't get worried or frightened. I could take that scattergun off your hoss right now and put both loads through your gut and all you'd do is fart buckshot."

"That's downright unnatural,"

"Ain't nothing about you natural from here on out. Walking and talking, while you should be sleeping with the worms and grubs six feet underground." Job strolled over to the campfire and picked up Joshua's gun belt. "Hope you don't mind, but I modified it. Cut the flap off and rigged the holster for a cross draw. Here, put it on. We're gonna try a thing or two."

Joshua took the belt from him and buckled it around his lean waist. The curved butt of the big Dragoon was angled across his lower belly to be drawn from the right. "You think I'm gonna be any better at this than I was before? I don't know many dearly departed that are spry enough to draw a six-gun with any accuracy and speed."

"Quit your belly-aching and do as I say." Job pointed fifty feet away. "See the knothole on that sour gum tree yonder? Let's see you put a single shot through it."

"Hell, I can scarcely make it out from here," Joshua complained. "Besides, just having one eyeball to see with throws me off a mite."

"You'll get accustomed to it. Besides, that blind one gives you a disturbing characteristic. Big and yellow and glowing in the dark of night...won't be no mistaking you with anyone else. An unnerving thing to look upon, it is."

The dead man shucked the forty-four from its holster and held it at arm's length. It was as true as the barrel of a cannon...steady and on the mark. He cocked the piece and fired. It recoiled with a thunderous boom and an eruption of flame and burnt powder.

"Did I get near it?"

Job took a brass spyglass from a leather bag on his belt. He extended the telescope and grinned. "Take a gander."

Joshua did, placing the eyepiece to his good orb. "Well, I'll be damned. It went clean through the center."

The black man took the spyglass from him. "Now, let's go a bit further. I want you to draw that hogleg as fast as you can and fan the hammer. This time straight from the hip. Put those remaining five slugs exactly where you put the first one."

"You're tetched in the head. Ain't no way I'm gonna be able to do that."

"Stop being such a mule-headed son of a bitch and do as I say!" snapped Job. "*Now!*"

It was like the dead man didn't even have to consider it. Nickled steel was suddenly clear of the holster and in his hand, while the other was fanning the spurred hammer in a pale-fleshed blur. In fact, the report of the gun didn't seem to be five at all, but only one.

Before he could return the Colt to its holster, Job was running toward the tree, cackling like a madman. "Whoo, boy! Get your cold, dead ass over here and see what you just done!"

Joshua walked over, a little slower than the black man had. When he got there, he scowled. There was only one puncture in the knothole of the tree.

"Well, that didn't turn out like you expected, did it?"

The mojo man laughed. "On the contrary!" He took a folding knife from his britches pocket and began to chisel at the knothole, holding his dark hand cupped underneath. Joshua watched as one...two...three...four...five round balls were extracted from the trunk of the sour gum. Before he was through, Job walked around to the opposite side, then emerged, his brown eyes twinkling. He had a lopsided lead ball between his thumb and forefinger. "And this makes number six!"

"So, you've made me into some sort of enchanted gunfighter," said the corpse in resignation. "Where is that gonna get us?"

"A far piece!" Job told him, annoyed with the man's ungratefulness. "If you're going to get your boy back, you can't be that sorry weakling of a fella you were when they brought you down. You can't be that man a'tall. Joshua Wingade is dead and gone."

Joshua was taken aback. "Now, come to think of it, how do you know my name? And about what they did to my wife and my promise to the boy, as well."

"Well, if'n you need to know, I was hiding in the woods when those fiends dealt you a losing hand…watching the whole time."

"And you didn't come out and help me?"

"I ain't the fool you were," Job told him. "The witch alone is a formidable adversary. You add an honest-to-goodness vampire and three minions conjured from the bowels of Hell… fatal adversaries for a mortal man to reckon with, for sure. But it's different now. They're playing on *your* terms now. Not a victim, but an equal. Immortal and unstoppable, with a gun hand as fast as greased lightning. An avenging angel named Dead-Eye."

The tall man stared at him blankly. "You gotta be funning me. I ain't calling myself that."

"Then *I'll* call you that! You can call yourself steaming dogshit on toasted sourdough for all I care. But Dead-Eye you are and will be from here on out."

The corpse in the black broadcloth suit shook his head wearily. *Lord, this fella can be a worrisome one!* "Fine. Whatever you say. Don't you think we oughta head on out if we're aiming to catch up with 'em?"

"My sentiment exactly!" Job marched over to the campfire and kicked dirt and pebbles over the flames until it was no more that smoke and ash. Then he dumped the dregs of the coffee pot on top of it and wrapped his essentials in his bedroll. "Our mounts are over yonder in that pine grove."

When they got there, Dead-Eye found his black Morgan tethered to a maple tree, grazing weeds. Next to it stood a pure white mule with a saddle and two canvas packs strapped to its hindquarters. Its eyes were as pink as a piglet slumbering in a bed of primrose and petunias.

"That your nag?" the gunslinger asked.

"That's my traveling buddy," Job told him. "His name is Balaam."

"Of course. Like that fella in the Bible with the talking donkey. Yours don't speak, does it?"

Job shrugged his narrow shoulders. "Ain't never said a word to me, but then maybe he never had anything worth saying. And what's your horse's name?"

"Name?" Dead-Eye puzzled over the question. "He ain't got one."

"Ain't decent neglecting your hoss like that," scolded the mojo man. "A trustworthy creature like that deserves a proper epithet. General Lee had Traveler and U.S. Grant had his Cincinnati. Call him Jack or Tom or even Mortimer. But call the poor animal something it can be proud of."

"Plain old 'horse' is good enough for me," said the Georgian. He walked up to the Morgan, stepped up into the left stirrup, and prepared to swing into the saddle.

Before he had a chance, the horse's eyes rolled in alarm and it snorted nervously as an unpleasant scent curled through its nostrils. It reared and bucked, tossing Dead-Eye a good twelve feet away. The dead man landed in a clump of blackberry bramble, looking none too pleased as he attempted to disengage himself from its thorny clutches.

"What the shit's the matter with him?" he demanded. He picked up his hat and started back toward the animal…and nearly received a hoof in the skull for his trouble.

"I was afraid of that," said Job. "He wants no part of you now."

"And why not?"

"Would you want something dead and decomposing strapped to your back for miles at a time?"

Dead-Eye shook his head in disgust. "So, what are we gonna do?"

The black man walked over to the gunfighter. "Let me borrow this for a moment," he said, yanking the Colt from Dead-Eye's holster. Then he stepped up to the Morgan and shot him squarely betwixt the eyes.

As the horse's legs collapsed and he fell heavily to his side, Dead-Eye was vexed to no end. "Why the devil did you do that?"

"Well, he weren't doing you no good the way he was," Job told him, handing him the sidearm. "We're gonna have to make him more agreeable to your condition." He went to one of the canvas packs and took several objects from its folds. The man then went to the horse, set four black candles to the north, east, south, and west of the carcass, and lit them with a sulfur match. Then he opened a small, leatherbound book and began to flip through the yellowed pages. The cover was wrinkled and tanned, and marred with what appeared to be freckles and moles.

"Looks a lot like the one the witch possessed," Dead-Eye told him.

Job was startled. "You've seen this book of hers?"

"No, but someone told me of it. Said she read from it, waving her hands, and opened a hole in the air."

"Lord have mercy!" exclaimed the mojo man, plainly disturbed. "Of all the confounded books, she'd have to tote that one with her!"

Dead-Eye began to suspect his resurrector wasn't being entirely truthful with him. "What do you know of this woman and the book she carries?"

"Let's just get this critter in the correct disposition and set to riding," said Job. "I'll tell you later. I promise you that."

Dead-Eye nodded and stepped back. The mojo man began to walk in a counter-clockwise direction, speaking words from the aged parchment of the little book. At first, nothing happened. Then the dead horse began to lurch and tremble. The whites of its eyes turned blood red, then fairly glowed like the grates of a potbelly stove stoked with kindling and tinder. A hoarse bellow rose from the animal's gullet and, with a leap, rose from the killing ground from which it had once lain as though a bolt of lightning had shot up its ass end. It shook its dark head violently, its muscles knotting and bunching beneath its coal black hide. Finally, it settled down and looked around. It eyed Job contemptuously, as though despising the man for the accursed state it was now in.

Dead-Eye knew that something was terribly amiss. "Now what the hell did you go and do this time?"

"Hell about sums it up," admitted Job, extinguishing the candles. He stowed them and the book back in the mule's pack. "I sorta conjured something to make your ride a little easier to handle."

Dead-Eye hated to ask. "Conjured *what?*"

Job grinned sheepishly. "Oh, weren't nothing but a demon of sorts, and a little bitty one at that. Just enough of one to make that contrary hoss of yours into one that doesn't give a damn whether you're dead or alive. Or anyone else, for that matter."

Dead-Eye approached the horse cautiously, but it no longer seemed adverse to his presence. He mounted it easily and sat tall in the saddle, half expecting it to throw him again. But it didn't. The black creature stood solid and steady beneath him, its muscles taut and ready to travel.

"Don't you worry," Job told him as he mounted Balaam. "Old Brimstone there will carry you through the gates of the netherworld and back. And, before we're through, it could very well come to that."

The gunfighter scowled. "Brimstone, huh? You're just a living, breathing dictionary full of names, ain't you?"

Job flashed his precious metal grin. "You're right about that. By the way, I've been meaning to ask...you don't have a powerful hankering for human flesh, do you?"

Dead-Eye considered it. "Can't say I have any appetite at all, now that you mention it."

"Good to know," the mojo man said, obviously relieved. "Zombifying can have that unfortunate effect from time to time. Eases my mind to know you won't be gnawing on my aged bones whist I sleep at night."

The gunfighter dug his heels into the flank of the Morgan, sending it out of the clearing and back onto the trail. "Quit your jawing and let's ride."

"You heard the man, Balaam," the mojo man told his mule. "Move your flea-bitten white ass, ass."

Together, they headed westward across the Tennessee countryside, aware that only darkness and danger lay ahead of them.

CHAPTER SEVEN

The Old Natchez Trace, South of Nashville
Mid-October 1866

They traveled west across Tennessee, past the town of Murfreesboro, until they reached a lonesome backroad across harvested pastureland. The countryside seemed tranquil, but the ugly wounds inflicted by Holland and his band of marauders could be plainly seen every so often. Atrocities that had been wantonly committed, and seemingly with no rhyme or reason at all.

Once they had spotted a huge, charred oak in the center of a field. They had left the trail to investigate and found that a farmer had been crucified there. His wrists and ankles had been hammered in place with iron spikes from the bowed limbs and the trunk. His feet had been doused with whiskey and then set aflame.

A few burnt coins that had fallen from the pockets of his consumed clothing lay on the ground. The motive had not been robbery. It had been for sick pleasure and a desire to inflict pain and horrifying death.

Dead-Eye and Job continued onward. They skirted the town of Franklin, keeping to the south. The gunfighter remembered the place; the skirmishes, the bloodshed, and his eventual capture. He also recalled the physical and mental cruelty he had suffered at the Yankee prison camp afterward. It no longer haunted him, though. One advantage of his condition was the utter lack of suffering emotionally over injustices of the past. The dead didn't fret about such things. The only thing that did remain foremost in his mind was the violation of his family...the rape and damning of his beloved Elizabeth and the abduction of Daniel. That was what drove him...what prevented him from digging a hole in the earth, lying down, and pulling the dirt in after him.

Vigilantly, they followed the tracks of the three riders and the horse-drawn wagon. There was a fifth horse, but its tracks were lighter in impression. Apparently, it was either a fresh mount or the vampire's horse during the nocturnal hours.

"He probably spends his days holed up in a casket inside the cabin of the wagon," Job sagely surmised. "One with a cushion of earth from his native country. From that accent, I'd say he was from Germany or thereabouts. I've always heard there were bad goings-on across the ocean. Nosferatu, they're called over there. A man in Shreveport once told me about a nobleman in a place called Transylvania in the Carpathian Mountains. Said he thrived off the drinking of human blood...that it kept him young, like a dipper of water from the Fountain of Youth. Said he had brides of the same persuasion, too."

Dead-Eye felt an ember smolder and glow hot in the center of his cold, gelatinous brain. By Holland's own admission, Elizabeth had been one of his many brides. Yet he had chosen to abduct the boy and abandon her to fend for herself. He recalled the thing she had become; defiant, cruel, and hungry with immortality. The Southerner attempted to remember her as she had been, that spring morning when he had departed for war. Delicate and tender, her eyes full of love and concern for the husband who she feared would never return home. But that image would not present itself. Only the earth-smeared, wicked thing with the mouthful of fangs and an unholy bloodlust in her eyes.

A couple of days later, they found where the outlaws had left the trail and headed northward along the rocky passageway of the Natchez Trace. "It's not used near as much as it was way back in the late 1700s and the beginning of this century," Job said. "It was a mighty busy trail back then, stretching from Nashville clear to Natchez, Mississippi. They said Andrew Jackson once marched an army of civilian soldiers—mostly Tennessee ridgerunners and Kaintucks—four thousand or more strong, down the Trace to battle the British at New Orleans. And the explorer Meriwether Lewis died of mysterious circumstances and was buried no more than a stone's throw from here. Some say he killed himself by his own hand, but others say he was brutally murdered."

Dead-Eye rode along, staring straight ahead, nodding amiably from time to time. If the black man liked to do anything, it was talk. And it was mostly to hear himself jabber about one subject or another, or some bizarre tidbit of knowledge or folklore he had picked up during his years of traveling.

Toward evening, they entered a dense stretch of forest. The trees at the sides of the trail bowed inward, their leafy branches intermingling until scarcely a bit of sunlight peeked through their dense boughs. In the gloom, the lonesome trail seemed downright disquieting.

Minutes later, they rounded a bend and stopped. Up ahead stood a chestnut brown mare by the side of the trail. Laying prone in the middle of the road was the body of a man. He was sprawled on his back, motionless, his head cocked rearward and his mouth wide open. He wore the white collar and black cassock of a traveling preacher.

The clothing was riddled with bullet holes and blood dyed his shirt a crusty reddish brown.

"Looks like he fell prey to some bad doings," said Dead-Eye. "Think it was Holland and his bunch?"

"Naw," Job told him. "He looks too damn good. Probably bandits. I hear tell they lay in wait from time to time."

Slowly, they approached the body in the road. Scattered about him was a straight-brimmed pastor's hat and a King James Bible. The brown mare continued to stand where it was, drinking from a mud puddle.

"Hold up," the mojo man said softly.

"What is it?"

"Something ain't right here. That hat and Bible...they look like they've been set about...not dropped. And that hoss ain't spooked or nothing. Like it's accustomed to this sort of situation."

Dead-Eye studied the man in the road. "You think he's playing possum? Maybe up to no good?"

"We'll just see about that." Job reached into one of his vest pockets and took out a tin snuff box. It looked as though he had taken a saddler's awl and punched holes in the cover. He removed the lid and lifted something out. It squirmed and twisted between the man's dark fingertips.

"What in tarnation is that?" asked Dead-Eye.

The black man leaned forward in his saddle and flung the thing toward the man's body. The thing flipped, tail over pincers, and landed on the man's neck. It scuddled along his throat, climbed the peak of his chin, and crawled across his cheek.

"It's an earwig."

The moment the ugly insect reached the fellow's ear and started squeezing inside, the gunshot preacher was off the ground in a flash. "Land sakes!" he screamed. "Get this damn thing off of me!" As he rose, the hand that had been folded behind his back came into view, holding a Colt Navy revolver.

"I'd heard tell that was just an old wives' tale," said Dead-Eye, "them critters crawling in folks ears."

"I reckon I can train a critter to do per near thing I want," Job proclaimed. "Be it a dog or a mule or an ugly, old pincher beetle!"

Before they knew it the woods came alive around them. One man burst from the trees on the right and one on the left, both on horseback and toting rifles. Another appeared behind them. He was on foot, holding a six-shot pepperbox pistol at arm's length.

"I knew there were pigeons in this pie," Job said. "They done gone and hornswoggled us!" As guns were raised and centered on him and Dead-Eye, the mojo man raised his hands to his shoulders in surrender. No one noticed he had slipped his boots from the stirrups of the mules saddle, nice and easy like.

The bandit in the preacher's getup bucked and jumped as he grappled with the thing hanging halfway out of his ear. He shrieked as he got hold of the tail and yanked it free. Its long, curved mandibles were slick with blood. Disgusted, he flung it off into the thicket beside the trail.

"Y'all aiming to rob us?" Dead-Eye asked, apparently unconcerned.

"You bet your ass we are!" said a big man atop a speckled gray. He settled the sights of a Henry rifle on the Southerner's chest. "And we're gonna take it all. Your horses, your guns, your duds…"

"Your lives, too, if you don't cooperate," the fellow with the pepperbox warned.

The preacher man with the .36 revolver had regained his composure, even though a trickle of blood ran past his earlobe and down his stubbled jaw. "What I'm a taking is this critter," he said, eyeing the black Morgan with a tobacco-stained grin. "Mighty prime piece of horseflesh, he is!"

Dead-Eye regarded the man with his one good eye. His pale face was impassive and untroubled. "If you want him...you'd best come over here and get him."

"Go on," suggested the horseman on the right. He was a wiry man with rusty red hair, and held a Merrill 54-caliber carbine in his hands. "If he makes one wrong move, we'll blow him out of the saddle."

With a swagger, Preacher walked up, reaching out for the horse's bridle.

A low, thunderous grumble rolled up from Brimstone's gullet.

Startled, the man stopped in mid-step. He looked up at Dead-Eye. "Did your horse...did he just...*growl* at me?"

The Southerner shrugged. "He don't cotton to strangers much."

"Well, confound the critter, he's sure as hell gonna cotton to me!" Without hesitation, he lashed out and slapped the animal violently across the side of the head. "Gonna show you who's..."

Before the word 'boss' could leave his lips, Brimstone promptly fastened his yellowed teeth around the preacher's throat and bit his head off.

"Thunderation!" cried the man with the Henry. His eyes widened as Preacher's head rolled, stump over scalp, and landed beneath his horse's hooves. Spooked, the animal bucked, causing the man to lose his rifle, fighting to stay in the saddle.

Dead-Eye turned his head to see the wiry fellow aiming the carbine square at him. The Dragoon was suddenly clear of its holster. The dead man fanned the hammer, filling the air with flash and burnt powder. The .54 musket dropped to the ground a moment later, as well as all five fingers of the bandit's hand.

To the right of Dead-Eye, Job dug his heels into Balaam's flanks. Without warning, the albino mule reared up and unleased a shrill hee-haw of alarm. The mojo man rolled backward with the momentum, flipped head over heels, and landed squarely on his feet, facing the outlaw behind him. Before the man could fire, Job tossed a fistful of gray powder into the man's eyes. Soon, the flesh around the bandit's eyes grew purple and began to swell shut. As he screamed and dropped to his knees, the black man pulled a narrow bladed knife from the cuff of his sleeve and ran the edge across the outlaw's throat with a single swipe. The man sputtered and strangled on his own blood, then fell backward and grew still.

A gunshot cracked and the mojo man turned to see Dead-Eye's left ear spin from his head and land in the dirt.

"Shitfire!" cussed the gunslinger. The man on the dapple had pulled a pistol after regaining his balance. Dead-Eye reached down and grabbed hold of the stock of the scattergun. He tugged, but the weapon was stuck in the scabbard. A second shot punched through the crown of the Southerner's hat. The bullet glanced forcefully off the dome of his skull, taking a furrow of lank hair and dead flesh with it.

Finally, the twelve gauge pulled free. Dead-Eye swung the shotgun up, cocking the curved hammers with the other hand. He squeezed both triggers simultaneously. Twin loads of double-aught buckshot hit the big man squarely in the ample gut. He was propelled backward from his saddle and landed in a crumpled heap, fifteen feet away.

Shaking his head woefully, Job walked over and picked up the dead man's ear. "I'll hold onto this for safe-keeping," he said sticking it in one of his vest pockets. "We'll sew it back on later. First, we gotta have a talk with that fellow yonder."

Dead-Eye swung down off Brimstone and, together, the two approached the wiry fellow with the red hair. He had fallen off his horse and was on the ground on his hands and knees, blubbering like a baby and gathering up his lost fingers. The Southerner hauled off and kicked the bandit in the ribs, causing him to flip onto his back with a groan. Job straddled the man's chest and had a seat, making himself comfortable. He took a pipe from his vest, filled the bowl with tobacco from his pouch, and lit it with a sulfur match.

"All right, now," said the black man after taking a puff. "Got a question or two to ask."

"I ain't telling you nothing, you filthy, little nig—"

Job wagged a dark finger in his face. "Hush it up now! You let that nasty word cross your lips and you'll be belching up nightcrawlers and shitting snakes for a week. And believe you me, I can make it happen, too!"

"I'd shut up and listen, if I was you," Dead-Eye advised. "Or he'll lay the hoodoo on you for sure."

Red noticed the collection of necklaces and charms hanging about the little man's neck and refrained from protesting any further.

"Fine," said Job. "Now let's get on with it. From the holes in that preacher's shirt, I take it the rightful owner is dead."

The fingerless outlaw scowled. "Chester, over yonder, done it. Filled that holy man with lead and shucked his clothes off'n him. Thought it was right funny…said it would be a right clever way to trick folks and take 'em off guard."

The mojo man looked over his shoulder. "Yeah, ol' Chester looks mighty clever, laying yonder with his head a dozen feet from his neckbone. What'd you do with the preacher man? Give him a decent burial?"

"Shit no! Covered him with leaves and left him where he laid."

"Treating a man of God like that could set a plague upon you or such," Job told him. He blew a lungful of tobacco smoke into the bandit's face, causing him to cough. "Ain't you afraid the Lord'll send lightning bolts upon your head?"

"Aw, them's just lies and tall tales!" spat Red. "I don't believe nary a thing about Heaven or Hell."

"You'd best be believing," said Job, "'cause there's hellspawn roaming this countryside at this very moment. Which leads me to my next question? Have you seen a gang ride through the Trace in the past day or so? Three men on horseback, maybe four, depending on the hour of the day or night? And a wagon painted black, drawn by two ebony horses? Maybe driven by a woman in dark garments?"

An uncomfortable look crossed Red's face, canceling the pain in his mangled hand for a moment. "Yeah...we seen 'em. Thought better than to give 'em a try, though. We'd heard talk about that white-haired feller and his men, and the godawful things they've done. And about the witch, too. It's said she came upon a traveling corset salesman in a saloon in Ringgold a while back. He got drunk on pop-skull and tried to force himself upon her. And she hauled off and turned him into a dad-blamed possum!"

Job nodded. "Yessir. I reckon she could do that, if'n she had a mind to."

"So, we laid low and let 'em pass. I didn't want them skewering me with a fence post, or eating me, or turning me into a critter or such."

"Did they head north for Nashville?"

"No. They went a ways, then took a turn west, heading the direction of Kingston Springs and White Bluff just beyond."

"Much obliged." Having gotten what he needed, Job stood up, allowing the outlaw to breath freely again.

"What do you want to do with him?" asked Dead-Eye. He dipped his hand into the side pocket of his frock coat and, taking out a powder flask, lead balls, and percussion caps, began to reload the Dragoon. "Put a bullet in his brain pan?"

Red's expression of terror turned into relief when Job shook his head. "I see no need in doing that without further provocation on his part." He regarded the bleeding stub with the missing five digits. "Would that be your gun hand?"

"It was."

"And you can't shoot well with the other?"

"Couldn't hit a privy door, even if I was sitting inside, taking a shit. To tell the truth, I was always a sorry hand with a gun. Usually let the others do the shooting for me."

Dead-Eye looked around at the carnage in the roadway. "Not anymore."

"I tell you what," said Job. "You climb on that there hoss and find you a quiet town. Take to something you can do one-handed…sweeping the courthouse steps or polishing spittoons in a gambling hall. Find you a good woman and have yourself a young'un or two. And get to believing in Heaven and Hell, 'cause there's a bit of both out there for a young feller like you. Just depends on which fork in the road you want to take."

Red nodded his thanks to the two, then scrambled for his horse. A moment later, he was in the saddle and galloping southward down the Trace.

Dead-Eye regarded his traveling partner with disdain. "Well, ain't you all rose pedals and velvet pillows today."

"You don't put much stock in second chances, I take it?"

"Not if they're for folks who want to rob me and leave me for the buzzards."

"Maybe I was just feeling generous for a change," said Job. "Normally, I'd be ready to drill the bastard like the rest of them."

Dead-Eye removed his hat and probed his scalp with his fingertips. He felt the bone of his skull in the pit of the furrow.

"Don't fret none. I can stitch that up when I sew on the ear," the black man told him. He walked over to the man whose throat he'd cut and picked up the pepperbox. He examined the firearm and stuck it in a vest pocket with the rest of his treasures. "Had trouble pulling that twelve-gauge from your saddle, didn't you?"

Dead-Eye nodded and returned his hat to his head. "The barrels kept binding up. I'll fix that when we get to the next town."

"We'll camp for the night a mile or two down the Trace, then head for Kingston Springs in the morning." Job grinned and patted the pocket that cradled Dead-Eye's severed ear. "I'll do my Frankenstein work before bedtime."

Dead-Eye nodded. "Best do it soon. It's kinda hard to hear with just a hole in the side of your head. Besides, my hat won't sit straight."

When they turned to prepare to ride out, they found the demon-horse had chewed open the bogus preacher's belly and was chomping on his entrails.

"Looks like Ol' Brimstone's got the man-eating hankering after all," Job observed. "Don't know if it's the zombie in him or the demon. Could be a little of both."

Dead-Eye swung atop the Morgan and yanked at the reins, attempting to pull the horse's muzzle out of the outlaw's abdomen. Brimstone's gore-covered face appeared with a kidney cradled greedily between his teeth. He swallowed the organ whole and dipped for another morsel, but his rider yanked his head away. The horse growled menacingly down deep in his throat.

"Don't take that tone with me, Beelzebub," the dead man warned.

"Wrong demon," said Job absently. He crouched down and took the discarded Bible in his hands, dusted it off. "His real name is forbidden to say aloud and a bitch to pronounce correctly if you did."

Dead-Eye watched as the mojo man stuck the holy tome in one of the mule's packs. "Didn't think you favored that old-time religion."

"Any book, good or bad, is deserving of respect."

"Excepting maybe that one the witch totes?"

The mojo man's eyes were as hard and grim as a tombstone as he mounted Balaam and urged him on down the Trace. "You have no idea how very right you are about that, my friend. If I had possession of the damned thing, I'd ride clear to the gates of Hell myself and hand deliver it to the flaming shithole from where it came."

And considering Job's solemn expression and the resolution in his voice, Dead-Eye knew he would do it in a heartbeat.

CHAPTER EIGHT

Kingston Springs, Tennessee
October 1866

Early the following morning, they rode into the town of Kingston Springs. It was a small, rural community located on the edge of the Harpeth River. Several businesses lined the street on both sides. To the left was a sheriff's office, hotel, livery stable, and doctor's office, while on the right, a general store, barber shop, saloon, and ladies dress shop. At the far end of the street, before the thoroughfare gave way to a scattering of simple houses, was a white-washed church and a schoolhouse. It was a crisp autumn morning. A silver whiskering of frost coated the grass and the roofs of the buildings, and the pungent scent of wood smoke from potbelly stoves and cooking ovens hung heavily in the air.

The first thing Dead-Eye and Job noticed was a gallows constructed of sturdy lumber in the center of the street. There were a number of townsfolk standing on the boardwalks and milling about in the street; more than there should have been at that early an hour.

"Looks like they've got a hanging planned," said Job.

"Don't seem none too happy about it, though," observed Dead-Eye. "Usually such proceedings are like a county fair. These folks look downright peeved."

"I'm heading to the store for coffee, pipe tobacco, and fiddle strings to replace the ones I cinched you up with. Are you in need of anything?"

"Gunpowder," said the gunslinger. "Forty-four round ball and shotgun shells, if'n they got 'em." He spotted the doctor's office and reined Brimstone in that direction. "You go on. I got business with the sawbones."

The black man eyed him suspiciously. "Now, what would *you* need a doctor for? A man in your condition?"

Dead-Eye ignored him and rode on. He swung down off the horse and tied the animal to a hitching post out front, then slid the shotgun from its scabbard. He didn't bother knocking on the door...just walked right in. Along with most of his compassion and tact, manners seemed to have been another social attribute he had forfeited during his transition from life to death.

The doctor, elderly and gray-haired, walked out of the back at the sound of his entering. The instant he saw the man in the long black coat, his eyes widened and he rushed forward. "Lord have mercy! Are you all right, man? You look to be half dead!"

That's an understatement, if there ever was one, thought Dead-Eye. "I ain't here for doctoring. I just need to borrow..."

But the physician would hear nothing of it. "Quickly! Come into my examination room! Maybe there is something we can do for you yet!" He grabbed the tall man by the arm and was shocked. "Good God, man! Your muscles have already atrophied! They're wasting away. I'm surprised you even had the strength to walk through that door!"

The doctor had ushered him halfway into the examination room, when Dead-Eye jerked his arm free from the man's grasp and glared at him. "Ain't nothing wrong with me! I'm healthy as a horse!" he lied. "Besides, I have need of something."

"And what would that be?"

"You got a bone saw?" he asked.

"I do. In my instrument cabinet over there. But what do you—?"

Dead-Eye pushed past the man, opened the glass-paned cabinet, and found what he was looking for. Bracing the length of the scattergun against the examination table, he began to saw the twin barrels away, eight inches above the double breeches.

The doctor was horrified. "Sir! That is a precision instrument! It is for the amputation of arms and legs!"

"So is this," the gunfighter told him, nodding toward the weapon, "if used properly."

After a minute or so of sawing, the barrels dropped to the floor with a clang. He then did the same with the walnut stock, cutting away the wood behind the curve of the wrist piece. "Y'all having a hanging today?"

The doctor grimaced angrily. "We were, but not now. Folks hereabouts are madder than hell! Had a local fella over in the jail...got stinking drunk one night and beat his wife and young'uns to death. He was to hang at precisely nine o'clock. But something happened last night that cheated the hangman."

"Did he escape?"

"No, he died in his sleep. A heart ailment, more than likely. The sheriff is fit to be tied and so is everyone else. Some folks traveled thirty miles or more for a front-row seat. They're of a nasty disposition and you can't blame them."

Dead-Eye finally finished his work. Satisfied, he abandoned the scraps of his labor, as well as the saw, and departed the doctor's office without so much as a 'thank you.'

He then walked over to the livery stable and purchased a set of reins. He tied one end of the leather securely around the stubs of the barrels and the other around the remaining wood of the stock.

"What in tarnation have you done there?" asked Job coming out of the mercantile with his purchases in hand.

"Saw a mountain Reb do this once. Chopped down a turkey gun and carried it under his coat on a sling. The buckshot spread was hellacious. Could take out three soldiers at a time, if they were close together."

"I've seen men cut near in half from a sawed-down twelve gauge." Job nodded back toward the store. "I left a couple more packages on the counter. Could you fetch 'em for me?"

Dead-Eye looped the sling of the scattergun around the horn of his saddle. With a sigh, he mounted the porch in front of the general store, intending to go inside. But, before he could enter, a large, broad-shouldered man came bustling out the door like a brahman bull charging out of a rodeo chute. He ran smack-dab into the lanky Southerner with enough force to throw him off balance, causing him to stumble off the porch and back into the street.

The fellow—one of many disgruntled citizens of Kingston Springs that morning—glared hatefully at the one that hindered him. "Best keep outta my path, stranger!" he barked. "Less'n you want me to put a hurting on you!"

"Oh shit!" proclaimed Job, spryly stepping around his mule to get out of harm's way.

Dead-Eye's one good eye narrowed, while the other remained wide, unseeing, and unnervingly bright within the shade of his hat brim. "If you aim to give it a try, there won't be no hurting a'tall on your part. Just the dark underside of a casket lid staring you in the face."

The big man's eyes fastened on the butt of the .44 jutting from beneath the folds of the Southerner's coat. "Fancy yourself as a gunman, do you? Well, no one's faster than Jake Hammond!" He eased his right hand backward, sweeping the cloth of his own coat to the side, revealing a holstered Lindsey twin-shot in a handmade holster. "Now, we'll count to three and draw. And since there's scarcely a yard betwixt us, one of us is gonna go down mighty fast and hard."

"You do the counting," suggested the Southerner. "I trust you."

Big Jake Hammond grinned. "All righty! One... Two..."

A bullet or two wouldn't smart worth a lick, thought Dead-Eye, his right hand lax and lazy beside his hip. *But I'll be damned if I'm gonna give that little banty rooster in the bowler hat another hole to stitch.*

Before Hammond could speak another number, the Dragoon was aimed right at him, belching smoke and lead. The bullet plugged the man squarely in the heart. He stood there, still flashing that smart-ass of his, unaware for a moment that he was already dead.

"Three," said Dead-Eye, reholstering his Colt.

He watched as Jake Hammond fell forward and noticed a hole in his back where the lead ball had gone clean through. Then he lifted his seeing eye and saw an elderly woman in a blue gingham dress and a Sunday-go-to-meeting hat standing a few feet inside the store. Her eyes were wide and startled as her hand slowly rose to her throat. She was quite a bit shorter than the man she had stood behind, so what had gone through his sternum and spine, had ended up in the middle of her gullet. Blood spurted through the cracks between her fingers and she crumpled into a heap, dropping a basket of eggs, slab bacon, and molasses she had purchased to surprise her husband at breakfast that morning.

Dead-Eye stared at her lifeless form for a moment, then shook his head. "Well, I'll be hog wallered."

"You'll be more than that!" yelled a man's voice from behind. Suddenly he was surrounded by angry hands; grabbing, punching, delivering violence and rage in one manner or another. One such hand grabbed the Dragoon and hauled it away out of sight and reach. More wrestled his arms behind his back and bound his wrists tightly together.

"He's done gone and kilt Granny Matthews!" the woman storekeeper wailed. "She's deader'n a ten-penny nail under a hailstorm of hammers!"

"Hang him!" yelled a tubby, freckle-faced boy. He took the escalating chaos as an opportunity to fill his pockets with peppermint sticks and licorice whips from the candy jars on the sales counter. "Hang the murdering bastard!"

No one seemed to notice the suggestion came from a child. The cry for hanging went up like a flock of blackbirds and took flight. Dead-Eye found himself hauled abruptly off his feet and lifted into the air. He caught a flash of angry faces and the empty gallows standing a hundred yards away. Without hesitation, he was carried off the boardwalk of the store porch and into the street, heading in that general direct. As his hat fell off, he caught an upside-down glimpse of Job standing there by Balaam, watching the whole thing transpire. The mojo man shrugged his narrow shoulders and silently mouthed *What do you expect me to do?* Dead-Eye held no hard feelings. He knew if the black man made a move to assist him, they would likely string him up, too…but from a tree and not a hand-built gallows.

It wasn't long before he was being toted up the steep steps to the execution platform. The crowd had grown from a dozen to forty strong. Even children were getting in on it, pelting him with rocks and calling him profane names, which was allowable, given the heat of the frenzy. A moment later, he was set, feet-first, upon the trap door in the floor and a noose of knotted hemp was looped around his throat.

"Hang him! Hang him! Hang him!" chanted the citizens of Kingston Springs and the friends and neighbors they had invited from neighboring towns and communities. Their faces were beet red and angry, but their eyes twinkled with an emotion akin to maniacal glee. It was plain to see that a cheerful mood had overcome them. Their morning wasn't a total waste after all.

No one asked him if he had any last words. No one prayed for his eternal soul or offered him a tow sack to pull over his head. "Now!" hollered someone. And, in response, the fellow elected as town hangman earned his dollar. He pulled the lever and the trapdoor fell away underneath.

Dead-Eye's lanky body dropped swiftly downward, then stopped abruptly with a brittle snap and a groan of protest from the timber beam that stretched above. Such a hooting and hollering and joyifying had never been heard in all your born days as the gathering gleaned cruel satisfaction from the tragic turn of events.

Folks jumped and danced—a few even did somersaults—as the tall man in the black broadcloth suit swung and spun lazily at the end of the noose. Then the celebration began to die down, replaced by confused muttering and fits of gap-mouthed silence. Eventually, all one could hear was the creaking of the taut rope...and the person who dangled at the end of it.

"What're you sumbitches gawking at?" Dead-Eye called down to them. "Ain't you ever heard a dead man talk before?"

The crowd dispersed with shrieks of fright and wails of alarm. Some even fainted and dropped where they stood. It wasn't long before the streets were empty. Even the sheriff and his deputies were out of sight. Doors were slammed shut, some even locked and bolted, and curtains were swiftly drawn.

Meanwhile, down the street, the dead man was swinging and swaying at the end of the rope, kicking and cussing up a blue streak.

Job picked up Dead-Eye's hat where it had fallen. He dusted it off and hung it on the horn of Brimstone's saddle with the sawed-off shotgun.

"Well...that went nicely."

Two days passed.

For forty-eight hours, by the light of day and the pitch of night, the corpse on the gallows cursed and complained, insulted and harangued the citizens of Kingston Springs.

Job had stuck around, but at a distance. He found a vacant lot behind the livery stable and set up camp there, keeping to himself and trying his best to stay out of folks' way. If they would hang a white man for an accidental shooting, they sure wouldn't think twice about doing the same to a sass-mouthed black man, especially with the tension and animosity generated by a Southern 'reconstruction'—as the Northern politicians called it—and wounds from a bitter civil war that were still a long ways from healing.

So, as he sat in the lot, he would cook him some beans and corn fritters, play himself a tune with the fiddle or Jew's harp, and keep Balaam fed with oats he bought from the livery man. Brimstone fended for himself, eating himself a stray dog or cat that wandered by every now and then.

On the morning of the third day, Job was sent for.

The one who came was the candy thief; the fat, little boy with the rash of freckles across his nose and cheeks. "I came to fetch you," the boy said, keeping his distance from the mojo man. Apparently, the townsfolk knew he had ridden in with the living dead man and were frightened of him about as much as they were of Dead-Eye.

"For what reason, boy?" asked Job, finishing up a breakfast of pan-fried biscuits and gooseberry preserves.

"They wanna talk to you about…you know, *him.*"

They both looked in the direction of the gallows. They could hear him clearly, cursing a group of church-going ladies, calling them a flock of "dried-up old whores."

"And who are *they*?" He offered the boy the last remaining biscuit and smatter of preserves. Hunger overrode fear, and the boy ambled up to the campfire, sat down, and eagerly took the food from the man's dark hand.

"The town council," the boy said, spitting crumbs. "Mayor McBride, Sheriff, Humphrey, the mortician Elias Sutton, and Pastor Jennings, the Baptist preacher. Oh, and Able Brown, the hangman. The whole thing's embarrassed the living shit out of him."

"Don't cuss, boy," Job told him. "Finish your biscuit and we'll be a-going."

"Can I have some coffee to go with it?" the youngster asked slyly. "Ma won't ever let me have any. Says it'll stunt my growth."

Job eyed the boy's girth. He poured a tin cup full and handed it to him. "Looks like you could use some stunting, if'n you ask me."

Fifteen minutes later, the boy left Job at the door of the one and only drinking establishment that Kingston Springs boasted. It was called the River's Bend Tavern and was rather fancified for a saloon in the sticks. It would have felt right at home in a town like Atlanta or New Orleans.

Job walked in, unannounced. The place was empty except for a big bartender with a handle-bar mustache and red garters on his sleeves, and a group of men at one of the circular gambling tables. Upon his arrival, they glanced around nervously, squirmed in their seats, and cleared their dry throats, despite the hard liquor they were downing at such an early hour.

"Come in and have a seat, Mister…uh…*Job*, is it?" said a broad, portly man with bushy gray muttonchops and a fifty dollar pair of duds. He was most likely Mayor McBride. From the familiarity of his features, it was an even bet that the candy-filching boy was one of his young'uns.

"It is," agreed the black man. He removed his derby hat and tossed it onto a brass hook by the front door. "And, if there is bourbon and beer involved, I will gladly sit a spell."

As Job crossed the barroom, the bartender's broad face grew more crimson by the moment. "Hell, Leonard!" he said, appealing to the town mayor. "You know very well that I don't allow no nigg—!"

The mojo man leveled a skinny, black finger at the man before he could finish his sentence. "You'd best keep that word locked tightly behind your teeth and out of my earshot!" he warned, giving the man the evil eye. He took the chicken foot from his collection of charms and made three circles in the air. "How'd you like a rash on your nether parts that won't go away for a month or two? Or a swollen nutsack you'd have to tote around in a wheelbarrow? Believe me... I can do either one...or both...if'n I have a mind to!"

The man's red face blanched of color and he failed to utter another word. Frightened, he went about his business and ignored the gathering at the table across the room.

Job sat in a chair reserved for him. He took out his pipe, tamped a wad of tobacco into the bowl, and lit it. The four men sat and watched him quietly as he reached over, grabbed a bottle of bourbon, and poured himself a shot glass full to the rim. He downed the liquor in one long, thirsty swallow. "Now, gentlemen...what is it that you wish to speak with me about?"

"You know very well what," said Sheriff Humphrey. The fellow was long and lean, with an Adam's apple prominent enough to hang a ten-gallon hat on. "*Him*...out yonder on the gallows."

"The one you executed without a proper and lawful trial?"

"But...but we *didn't* execute him," said a somber, dark-suited man that must have been Sutton the mortician. "Not really. Or he wouldn't be out there...like *that*."

"Oh, you executed him, all right," Job said. He reached over and took the undertaker's beer. He took a swallow and grimaced. It was lukewarm and flat. "Any normal man would be dead and buried by now. But seeing as Dead-Eye is already of the deceased persuasion…well, it just went and pissed him off in an almighty powerful way."

"Dead?" asked the preacher. His eyes regarded the black man distastefully. "That's rubbish, pure and simple. No one's been resurrected from the grave except our Lord and Savior Jesus after his crucifixion at Golgotha."

Job puffed on his pipe and blew a blue cloud across the table, causing Pastor Jennings to cough and wheeze. "Now, now, your holiness. You're a mite rusty on your Bible stories there. Shall we discuss the Old Testament or the New? Elijah raised the widow of Zarephath's son and the child of the Shunammite woman from the dead. And Christ Himself resurrected Jairus' daughter and Lazarus after he'd been a-stinking in the tomb for three days solid. And let's not forget the bodies of many holy folks, raised to life after Jesus's reappearance, who came out of the tombs and appeared to the multitudes in Jerusalem."

The preacher was not impressed. "Even Lucifer can quote scripture. If this man on the gallows is dead, yet reanimated, are you the one responsible?"

"Oh, most certainly."

"Then witchcraft is involved!"

Job rolled his eyes in exasperation. "Not quite. More like voodoo… You know, island sorcery. Potions and charms and spells and such. I've got a genuine mojo hand stashed in my bedroll if'n you'd like to take a gander at it."

The preacher seemed unsettled at the thought of looking upon such a thing.

"What we're wanting to know, Mister Job," said Mayor McBride, "is can you solve our little problem? You rode in with that fellow…that Dead-Eye. Can you ride on out of here with him as well? And never pass this way again?"

"Why don't you walk out yonder and cut him down yourself?"

"Well, frankly," said Able Brown, the hangman, who had been quietly pickling himself with rotgut the whole time. "Everyone in town is scared to death to go near him."

"And rightfully so," Job told the five. "He's a fearsome one to tangle with. I'd have to cast a spell and return him to his lifeless state my own self, just to remove him and tote him away. If not, he might turn on me for failing to help him and letting y'all manhandle him the way you did. But if I were to do so, there would have to be monetary remuneration involved."

"We've already discussed that amongst ourselves," assured the mayor. "We can pay you fifty dollars in gold coin to take him off our hands."

Job stared at them for a moment, then burst out laughing. "Really, gentleman! I'd take no less than three hundred dollars to do what you ask."

"That's preposterous!" scoffed the pastor. "Not only are you a purveyor of black magic, but a charlatan and thief as well!"

"All right then," said the black man, scooting his chair back. "I reckon I'll just pack up my necessities and be on my way…all by my lonesome. I'll leave ol' Dead-Eye to keep you company. Who knows? He might settle down and behave himself in two or three years…"

The five looked at one another, desperation making a mutual decision without a single word being uttered. "Very well, Mister Job!" said the mayor. "I reckon you've got us over a barrel." The five council members—the pastor included—pooled their resources and, soon, three hundred dollars in gold coins were shoved across the table toward the little black man.

"Much obliged, gentlemen," Job said with a grin. "'Twas a pleasure doing business with you. Now, if you'll excuse me, I must do the job I've been hired for and leave this charming town behind. But, first, I need my friend's pistol back. It was taken from him during the time of his unfortunate lynching."

The word obviously made the town council uncomfortable. They all knew emotions had been high that morning and the unintentional death of Granny Matthews had only added fuel to the fire. They considered Kingston Springs a God-fearing, charitable community and, during the morning of the hanging, they had managed to besmirch their reputation in a very ugly and lasting way.

The town sheriff reached beneath his coat and brought out the big, nickel-plated Colt. He shoved the Dragoon across the tabletop with a scowl of disgust.

Job promptly picked it up and stuck it in his belt. He stood up, downed one more shot of bourbon, and then brushed the three hundred in gold into a small leather bag he took from a vest pocket. With the pipe clutched firmly between his precious metal teeth, he walked to the saloon door and retrieved his hat. Then out the door he went.

A short while later, the five members of the Kingston Springs town council stood at the big window of the River's Bend and watched as the mojo man rode down the street on his mule, leading the gunfighter's black horse behind him.

Job stopped at the gallows and stood there for a moment, observing his traveling companion thoughtfully. All the time, Dead-Eye was cursing and complaining. The black man went to one of the mule's packs and withdrew a small, ornamental box of tarnished brass. He mounted the stairs to the platform of the gallows and positioned the box directly beneath the feet of the hanging man. Crouching, he lifted a lid speckled with holes and lit something inside. As he distanced himself on the stairs, a plume of noxious green smoke billowed from the box and completely engulfed the struggling gunfighter. A minute passed. When the vapor finally dissipated, Dead-Eye was motionless. Job shimmied up the post of the gallows, scooted on his belly across the upper crossbeam, and, taking a knife from his sleeve, cut the rope. The dead man fell heavily and landed on the floor of the platform.

They watched as Job dragged Dead-Eye down the stairs by his ankles, allowing his head to bump and bang against the risers on the way down. Then, with some effort, he flung the corpse across the saddle of the black horse and tied him down securely.

"Good riddance," said the undertaker as they began to leave the town limits.

"We must treat this as a cautionary tale," Pastor Jennings told them. "To be slow to anger and avoid such poisonous pitfalls in the future. Especially where swamp sorcerers and walking dead folks are concerned."

"Amen to that, brother," Mayor McBride told him. "Now let's pray for divine guidance. Then have another shot of hooch or two."

A quarter mile outside of town, Dead-Eye finally spoke.

"What in tarnation did you do to me? I can't move a muscle!"

"Just something I concocted from cypress root, bladderwort, gator piss, and wasp venom. When you set it afire, it puts out a paralyzing vapor. Makes you limp as a drunken snake and utterly useless for an hour or so. I'd say you still have a ways to go, so just relax and enjoy the ride for a while. And count your blessings we escaped that fiasco by the skin of our teeth."

"How'd you manage to talk them into letting you take me down?"

"You did that yourself with all your caterwauling and carrying on! Plus, they paid me to do it. Three hundred bucks traveling money to help us on our way!"

"Where do you think Holland and his gang are now?"

"It's difficult to say," Job told him. "I'm thinking they skirted the town we just left. Nobody there said anything about them and I'm pretty damn sure they would've if they'd passed through. They may be laying low. Could be they know we're after them. I've heard the witch, Evangeline, has the power to shine. You know, seeing the past, present, and future."

"Do you actually believe in such?"

"I certainly do!" declared the mojo man. "I'd think you would, too, given the dark and devilish things you've witnessed in the past few weeks."

"You think we'll catch up to them soon?"

Job stared sternly down the trail ahead of them. "I'm hoping and praying that we'll be catching up to them at all. From the way I see it, they're heading due west as the crow flies. If they make it past the Mississippi River, we'll have a troublesome time keeping 'em in our sights. That's mighty wide-open country out yonder. The Devil's Playground, some call it. A place you could lose yourself in and do whatever the hell you had a mind to do, with no one to answer to…not even the good Lord Himself."

CHAPTER NINE

An Unknown Territory in Central Tennessee
Late-October 1866

Several days following the incident at Kingston Springs, Dead-Eye and Job found themselves leaving the rolling hills and grassy pastures, and entering a stretch of dense woodland and thicket. As they reined Brimstone and Balaam along the trail and into the encroaching shadows within the thick-grown trees, something peculiar happened. A dark sensation began to creep through them slowly…a pall of heavy disquiet and foreboding, as though something within the midst of the forest and even beyond was terribly amiss. It was a thing that was both physical and mental in nature…and, yes, even vexing to a man's very soul. It was a mood felt by the animals beneath them as well.

Dead-Eye frowned. "Is it just because I'm dead, or has it gotten colder since we've rode into these woods?"

"Oh, I feel it, too," admitted Job. "There's definitely a chill about the place. And have you noticed? Everything is darker…the leaves, the bark of the trees, the earth. It all seems dreadfully *wrong.* Like this land is cursed with the taint of iniquity."

Something screamed in the treetops overhead. It sounded like a cross between a bird and a bobcat, maybe with a little human woman thrown in for good measure. They looked up and caught a fleeting glimpse of something leaping from one branch to another. It was nothing either of them could successfully identify.

Riding onward, they approached a fork in the road. One way led further west. The other headed due east and was marked with a weathered sign that bore a single word: BRIMSTONE. Dead-Eye's black Morgan halted in mid-stride and regarded the sign for a thoughtful moment, then started in that direction. The gunfighter had to jerk the reins forcefully to put the horse back on the right track.

"You didn't say he could read."

"I said he was a little demon," the black man told him. "Not an ignorant one."

They continued through the dark woods, cautious and on edge. Even Brimstone and Balaam were skittish. Both moved quicker than usual, as if eager to take leave of the cursed place.

A mile or so further, they began to realize they weren't alone. Faint rustling in the lush kudzu and thorny bramble at the sides of the trail told them they were being matched, step for step.

"We're being followed."

Job's hand snaked beneath his bowler and scratched his bald head. His eyes narrowed a bit. "Or stalked."

Dead-Eye grumbled to himself and shucked his Dragoon from its holster. "Damn if it don't take a helluva lot to spook a corpse...but spooked I am."

"Steady," the mojo man told him. "Don't go touching that thing off until we know what we're dealing with."

A moment later, they found out.

They heard the scrabble of footsteps in the dirt of the road behind them and turned around. What they saw both perplexed and startled them.

"What in Sam Hill is that thing?" asked Dead-Eye. The ball of his thumb caressed the spur of the Colt's hammer.

Job studied it for a moment. The thing was long, black, and low to the ground. It had no coat of fur. Instead, its body—lean torso, nimble legs, and a long tail—was covered in thick, black scales. Its head was slender and serpentine in nature, and its eyes were large and a peculiar shade of yellowish-green. As the two stared at it, it stared back, stone still in the center of the road.

"I'd say it's a critter that's part dog and part snake," Job told him. "And one that's downright contrary and unpredictable, if I were to take a wild guess."

"Well, it ain't nothing a'tall now." Dead-Eye cocked the revolver's hammer and took aim at the thing in the road. It simply glared at him and, from deep down in its gullet, a staccato of dry hissing escaped. It almost sounded like the thing was laughing.

"Now, do you really think that pea-shooter's gonna put a dent in that brute?" Job asked him.

Dead-Eye scowled. He holstered the Dragoon and reached under the tails of his coat to retrieve the sawed-off twelve-gauge.

"Uh-uh. I'd bet you a twenty dollar gold piece that a blast of buckshot would rattle off that thing's scales like a spring rain off a tin roof." Job eyed the creature carefully and a look of dawning realization crossed his dark face. "Anyway, we don't possess the type of ammunition it takes to defeat this abomination."

The snake-critter seemed to understand the man's words. A wicked grin split its scaly face, displaying narrow, yellow teeth as long as tent stakes. The creature added emphasis to its action by displaying a long gray tongue that was forked in the middle. The appendage swept slowly across its fangs, as though Old Scratch himself had just rung a supper bell in Hell.

"So, you're thinking you know where we are…and what this critter might be?"

"Yessir. I am, indeed, of that inclination." Job looked as though a mood of uneasy introspection had taken hold of him. "I've heard tales before of a county in these parts that's not of the norm. A spot that's depraved and malevolent…as though Mephistopheles himself had vomited and stirred the nastiness around, and left it to sprout and grow a garden of unfettered evil. I never knew the name of the place, for decent folk refused to talk of it. All I know is that the mere mention struck a dark and secret terror in their hearts. It's a fearful territory, or so I've heard."

"And this monstrosity that dogs our heels?"

"One of many miscreations that dwell here. You but only have to look around to see what it's capable of." Job lifted his eyes toward the tops of the trees and nodded. "Like that yonder."

Dead-Eye followed his gaze. Amid the upper branches of the dark trees, nestled in shadows, were cocoons. Not the chrysalis of moths and butterflies, but ones massive enough to contain much larger occupants. One was the size of a small child, while another could have encased a grown man. A third was even larger. From the walls of the last pod protruded the antlers of a good-sized deer.

The gunfighter thought of the substance that had entrapped Marshal Bradley and his posse. *Could this thing be the devil Bradley talked of?* wondered Dead-Eye. *The fiend called Mymahthu?* But as he examined the cocoons further, he determined that what held the critter's prey was the shed skin of its own body, wrapped tightly, strand upon strand, until there was no chance of escape. A rancid stench curled through his nostrils. It was one he had smelled before; the pungent bitterness of a den of serpents…yet contained in a single, corrupt being.

"Let's move slowly down the trail," Job suggested. "Maybe it'll go about its business and leave us be."

Dead-Eye jerked the reins, causing Brimstone to whirl toward the western end of the road.

"*Slowly*, you imbecile!" Job warned beneath his breath. "You take off at a gallop and the thing will make sport and run you down. Then it'll be you and your hoss trussed up there in the treetops."

Leisurely, they began to continue through the forest. From the distance, the snake-critter followed, low to the ground, like a freakish snake that had sprouted limbs and was no longer allowed to slither on its belly. Every now and then, its putrid eyes would narrow and that husky, rattling laugh would rumble in its throat. And saliva mixed with venom would drip past black gums, squeeze through the gaps between its jagged teeth, and spatter upon the earth.

"You recall that story I told you?" Dead-Eye said, looking over at his companion. "About the thing that defeated that lawman and his deputies? The beast called Mymahthu? Do you think this one came from the same place?"

"I don't believe so," Job told him. "I have a feeling this critter has lived here a very long time...and that he is not the only one of his kind."

They rode another mile further and, from a distance, could see an opening in the timberline. A broad, warm swath of bright sunlight beckoned to them. The riders and their mounts yearned to be there, but they knew they mustn't rush to get there. As maddening as it was, they kept to their easy pace, resisting the urge to break and run.

When they were no more than a dozen yards from the border between darkness and light, the creature made its move. It leapt forward like a streak of greased, black lightning, veering quickly to the right.

"Watch out!" cried Job. He tightened his thighs around the saddle, as Balaam bucked with alarm. The snake-critter's mouth yawned wide, displaying that wicked picket of poisonous fangs. It dipped low to the earth, intending to take the mule's hooves off at the ankles and send the mojo man tumbling to the ground.

Before it could, however, a flash of blackness lashed out. There was a metallic *clang* as one of Brimstone's shoed hooves planted itself between the monster's yellow eyes. The force of the blow sent it rolling, snout over tail, fifty feet back down the trail.

"Whoa, boy!" Dead-Eye attempted to rein the Morgan around, but its demon half would have nothing of it. As the snake-critter rose to its feet, glossy back arched in defiance, Brimstone unleased a noise unlike any that either man had ever heard before. It was a harrowing battle cry from a place where such cries are commonplace, brimming with hatred and fatality. The demon horse's mouth opened and, from within its hollow, the crimson of infernal cinders glowed, stoked as hot as hellfire. Brimstone's eyes took on the same Hadean hue and Dead-Eye could feel the mount grow warm beneath him, as though he might combust and explode at any moment.

The snake-critter was a seasoned slayer and not one that lost nerve in the face of resistance. But it had never, during its existence in the dark forest of the evil county, encountered an adversary such as this. It gave one last hiss of disdain, then slithered up the dark column of a gnarled oak tree and was soon gone from sight.

"Well, I'll be damned," Job said softly. "Looks like I went and conjured up a fit leviathan after all."

Dead-Eye leaned forward and patted his horse atop the head. "Good boy," he said in approval. But the steed was still as hot as a poker and the dead man's palm came away scorched and blistered.

A trot and a gallop later, they had broken free of the ungodly land and found themselves bathed in bright sunlight. In comparison, the warm rays nearly blinded them. But their spirits lifted and grew lighter, casting off the somber and oppressive disposition that the evil territory's atmosphere had laid upon their hearts and minds during their uneasy journey.

CHAPTER TEN

Camden, Tennessee
Late-October 1866

The following afternoon, the two reached the town of Camden. The moment they rode down the main street, they knew something was amiss. There was tension in the air, but not the same sort they had experienced in Kingston Springs. From the expressions upon the faces of the townsfolk, it was plain to see they had been terribly disturbed by something. Something they could not rightfully understand or had no solution in resolving.

"What goes on here?" asked Dead-Eye. They paused by the open door of Ansel's Livery Stable, where a lean, rawboned man in a sooty shirt and scorched leather apron beat a horseshoe out of red-hot iron with the aid of a mallet and anvil.

"There have been doings of an abominable nature performed at the church house yonder," he said with a thick Swedish accent. "Witchery like nothing we have ever laid eyes upon! Perplexing to look upon and even more inconceivable to consider."

Job glanced down the street and saw several men standing around the steps of the steepled church. They seemed worried and at a loss of what to do. The mojo man's eyes narrowed. "This witchery...did it involve a dark-skinned woman dressed in black?"

The smithy's eyes widened. "Indeed, it did! Do you know of this enchantress?"

The black man frowned sourly and nodded. "We've crossed paths from time to time." He looked back toward the church house. "I reckon we'd best go and offer our services."

As he and Dead-Eye sauntered down the main street, the gunfighter eyed Job curiously. "What can we do?"

"You can't do a damn thing. But maybe I can undo the damage she's caused, whatever it may be."

When they reached the building, the men around the steps turned and regarded them with suspicion. A short, elderly man with a sheriff's badge pinned to the left gallus of his suspenders, spat contemptuously in the dirt. "Who the hell are you? And what do you want?"

"Perhaps to help," Job said, swinging down from Balaam's saddle. "I hear some wicked conjuring has been done in this place."

A rotund gentleman in the white apron and sleeve garters of a storekeeper stepped forward. "It certainly has! Two days ago. But we have no idea how to remedy it! It's beyond our comprehension, to say the least."

"What did the witch do?" Job asked.

A nerve at the corner of the sheriff's eye twitched. "Not being a churchgoer myself, I failed to witness it with my own eyes. But Clancy here did, from his property across the road."

Clancy was a tall fellow dressed in work clothing, wearing a brown felt hat. "I was sitting upon my porch on Sunday night, nigh around seven o'clock. The congregation was having a singing and, on around about the fourth hymn, four men on horses and a woman driving a black wagon pulled up out front. The lady looked infuriated about that singing, as though it were a personal offense to her. The horsemen waited while she left the wagon seat and mounted the church steps. She reached within a satchel slung across her shoulder and retrieved a book. Then she walked inside and closed the door behind her."

"What happened then?" asked Job.

"Well now, that singing stopped all of a sudden. I could hear the pastor admonishing her with that big, blustery voice of his, then other men of the congregation joined in with protests of their own. Then, abruptly, it stopped. Weren't nothing but silence. Then that woman in black left the church, shut the door behind her, and went back to her wagon. The others she was with laughed about the whole ordeal— except for a tall feller with white hair. He just sat on his horse and smiled the whole time. Then, together, they rode onward, heading west out of town."

Job turned back to the lawman. "May we go in?"

"I reckon there'd be no harm in having you take a look," he said. "I'll accompany you, even though it raises my hackles to lay eyes upon such evil doings."

Job and Dead-Eye followed the sheriff up the steps. The old man opened the door to allow them entrance. The moment they stepped inside the vestibule, they knew the witch named Evangeline had bewitched the congregation of Camden Presbyterian Church in a way that was difficult to understand or even believe, at first glimpse.

The pastor—a willowy man with spectacles and white jowl whiskers—stood at his pulpit, an accusing finger aimed at a point midway down the center aisle. In the wooden pews to the left and right sat several dozen citizens. Their faces were stricken with terror and dread. Four men had stood up and drawn their revolvers. Their guns were aimed at the same spot the preacher had been pointing at. The firearms were cocked, as though preparing to fire.

The peculiar thing about the entire affair was that they were frozen to the spot like statues. Unable to move from where they sat or stood.

"Lord have mercy!" said the sheriff, removing his hat, as if in reverence. "Precisely what did she do to these poor folks?"

Curiously, Job walked from one parishioner to another. He examined each carefully. He took one of the tiny glass bottles that hung around his neck and lifted it to the nostrils of a woman clutching a cowering child to her chest. When the glass misted over, he nodded and returned to where Dead-Eye and the sheriff stood.

"They are alive," he told them. "All of them."

"But...but why aren't they *moving*?"

"Time has been slowed down for them," he explained. "Slowed down to a point where they exist, but don't function at the same speed as we do. A minute for us is like a year to these poor souls. Mighty powerful magic she dealt out."

"But why?" asked the sheriff. "Why'd she do such a thing?"

Job flashed a crooked grin. "It was probably the hymn-singing. The sound of all that heavenly worship coming from one place exasperated the unholy hell out of her."

"Can you fix 'em?" asked Dead-Eye.

Job nodded. "I've reversed spells like this before, but not of such a magnitude." He took a pocket watch from one of pouches on his vest. He studied it, then lifted his eyes and surveyed the congregation around him. "This here timepiece ain't gonna cut it. Got to have something larger." He looked over at the sheriff. "You got a grandfather clock hereabouts somewhere."

"I do believe Clancy's wife has one in her parlor."

Soon, the sheriff, storekeeper, and the one named Clancy was hauling a tall clock of dark cherrywood and brass mechanisms up the church house steps and down the aisle. Job directed them to position it in front of the pastor's pulpit. Before he set to work, however, he eyed the four men who stood there with their drawn pistols extended at armlength.

"Let's move these gents around," he suggested. "When the spell they're under takes leave, they're liable to commence to firing...and shoot each other or anyone else in the crossfire."

The three townsmen and Dead-Eye began to move the four men from their spots.

"Damn!" cussed the storekeeper. "They're heavier than lead and stiffer than an old maid's corset!"

After some wrestling, they faced the men—and their pistols— away from the crowd and each other, and toward the stained glass windows of the sanctuary.

"Y'all wait by the door yonder," Job told them. He walked up to the grandfather clock and opened the glass door of the clockface, providing access to the ornate hour and minute hands. "Things are gonna get downright rambunctious in the blink of an eye and you're liable to get hurt if you're standing in the wrong spot."

They did as he requested. The four watched as he took the small, hide-bound book from his vest pocket and flipped a few yellowed pages, searching for the one he needed. When it was found, he began to read from the page in an unknown tongue, slowly raising his voice from a whisper to a full-blown shout. At the same time, he turned the hands of the grandfather clock with the dark fingers of his right hand. The words in the book seemed to take hold and the brass face of the clock changed from burnished yellow to furnace red. He snatched his hand away and the hands continued to spin on their own accord; slowly at first, then gaining in momentum. It wasn't long before they were turning so swiftly that they appeared as a blur and nothing more. At the same time, the pendulum in the belly of the clock swung to and fro, drumming like a tom-tom within its cabinet, causing the glass of the narrow door to fissure and shatter.

"Hold onto your hats, gentlemen!" he hollered, then plastered himself, belly down, across the boards of the church house floor.

At first, nothing seemed to happen. Then, gradually, they could detect small movements among the members of the congregation. The snail-paced flinching of a muscle, the near imperceptible blinking of an eyelid, a low, slow moan that began to mount in volume and turn into a gathering crescendo of shouts, cries, and exclamations. The occupants of the church came to full life thirty seconds later. The pistols of the four men went off, almost as one deafening report, blasting the colored glass from the arched frames of the windows they were directed at. Several hymn books took flight from angry parishioners, thrown with such force and fury, they would have nearly decapitated the mojo man if he had been standing.

With a great rush of sound and motion, all thirty-seven members of the Camden Presbyterian Church were back to normal. Women screamed, babies squalled, and men cussed, despite the fact that they were in a house of the Lord.

The pastor—his finger still extended and full of righteous condemnation—glared at a spot midway down the center aisle, his eyes fairly bulging from the sockets. Abruptly, an expression of utter dismay crossed his lean face. "Where…where did the harlot go?"

"She's been gone for a while now, preacher," Job told him, rising to his feet and returning his derby to his bald head. "You'd best save that accusing finger for next Sunday's service."

The man named Clancy walked down the aisle to where his wife's treasured grandfather clock stood. Its face was blackened, and the hands were smoldering and curled into charred bits of tin. The pendulum hung askew within its damaged chamber, battered beyond repair. "Opal Mae is gonna nail my hide to the barn door for this!"

After the members of the congregation had settled down, their thankfulness and generosity became bountiful and they passed the collection plate around. At the end of the last pew, it boasted fifty-three dollars in gold coin. The offering was ceremoniously presented to their dark-skinned savior for the blessings he had bestowed upon them. He neglected to inform them that their deliverance had been conjured by swamp voodoo and black magic of the most ungodly kind imaginable.

After they had walked out and swung atop their mounts, Job deposited the gold in his money bag, which still bulged with the bounty given to him by the disgruntled citizens of Kingston Springs.

As they continued westward up the trail, Dead-Eye regarded his traveling partner with begrudging admiration. "You sure have a mighty peculiar way of earning a dollar," he told him.

CHAPTER ELEVEN

On a Farm near Skullbone, Tennessee
Late-October 1866

For fifty miles, west of Camden, they rode, across wooded hills and vast expanses of recently-harvested farmland. Every now and then, Job would spot a tree standing amid a grove of others and pause for a while. Taking a hatchet from one of Balaam's side packs, he would chop a leafless branch or limb away and lash it securely to the haunches of the mule.

"It's not often you come upon an ash tree," the mojo man explained. "In our situation, each one is as valuable as gold in the pocket."

When they camped for the night, Job took the folding knife from his britches pocket and commenced to whittling. As the night sky blackened and his dark face was etched in the orange glow of the campfire, the mojo man would lay the objects of his labor upon the ground beside him. Twenty-four ash wood bullets of 44-caliber for Dead-Eye's Colt Dragoon, an equal number of 36-caliber projectiles for the pepperbox he had taken from the body of the throat-slit outlaw on the Natchez Trace.

"Hand me six of those shotgun shells," he requested of the zombie. Dead-Eye took a handful of brass casings and tossed them to the black man. Job pried open the ends of the shells with the tip of his knife, emptied the shot out of the recess above the powder, and replaced it with a plug of ash wood as big as his thumb. Closing the ends, he gave them back to the gunfighter. "Keep those handy in your coat pocket. You may have need of them when we catch up with Holland and his gang. We'll make paper cartridges with the bullets, so you can load that big hogleg of yours in a pinch, if you have need to."

"What about the three who ride with him?" Dead-Eye asked. "The ones called Rooster, Boar, and Snake? Will ash take them down as well?"

"Maybe. Just depends on what sort of fiend they are and where they originate from," said Job. "More than likely, pure silver will destroy them, but that's not written in stone."

"Now, how the hell are you gonna get silver bullets?"

The mojo man grinned. His precious metal teeth gleamed and glinted in the firelight. "Got silverware stashed in my provisions— forks, spoons, and such—for melting down and pouring in a bullet mold of your caliber that I have on hand." He patted the small, leather-bound book in his vest pocket. "And I have this, for when we need more than wood and silver to fight with…and when I finally face Evangeline. And it's inevitable that I will…sooner or later."

Job grew silent as he continued to work with the knife, shaving ash wood stakes to wickedly-sharp points. Dead-Eye studied the man's face and found it solemn and troubled.

Does he fear this witch? wondered the gunslinger. *Is he afraid that he is no match for her? Perhaps her magic is more potent than the kind he's versed at conjuring. If that's true, then God help us both.*

Late the following evening, they came upon a crossroads. A wooden sign that stood at their junction showed the names of two towns. To the northwest was PALMERSVILLE, while to the southwest was SKULLBONE.

"Wonder what sort of sordid history brought about the naming of that town?" asked Dead-Eye.

"No telling what we'll be finding there," Job replied. "I'd say the vampire and his disciples wouldn't be able to resist a place like that."

They took the left-hand trail. Overhead, dark clouds hung like mats of dirty cotton; boiling turbulently, promising rain and thunderous fury. The two riders quickened their pace, watching for someplace suitable to pitch camp for the night.

They were scarcely a mile past the road sign, when rain began to pelt them. It came gently at first, dampening their hats and clothing. Then lightning flashed overhead and, with a booming thunderclap, the heavens opened up. Raindrops grew fast and plentiful, and it wasn't long before they found themselves in the middle of a downpour.

"Yonder!" called Job, pointing toward a farm at the side of the road. Dead-Eye regarded the two-story farmhouse and the gathering of outbuildings that surrounded it. They all were dark and deserted. Nary a light shown from any of the windows of the dwelling. "Let's head for that barn!"

The animals beneath them headed toward the vast structure of their own accord. Brimstone and Balaam hopped a split-rail fence and galloped for the open doorway of the weathered barn. By the time they were out of the storm and safely within the shelter of the building's hollow, both Dead-Eye and Job were pert near soaked to the skin.

Even inside, the rain followed, blowing through the opening by a boisterous wind. "Shut and bar those doors!" the mojo man instructed. Dead-Eye did as he instructed, pulling both doors closed and securing them with a length of hewn lumber fashioned for that purpose.

For a moment, they stood in the gloom, attempting to make out their surroundings. Job located a coal oil lantern hanging from an overhead beam and lit it with a sulfur match from a vest pocket. The golden glow showed sacks of feed, farming implements such as hoes, rakes, and pitchforks, and a wooden ladder that led to a loft above. Further within the structure were twin rows of stables cloaked in shadow.

"Looks like this is where we'll be setting camp for the night," said Dead-Eye. Thunder and lightning raged overhead and the cedar shingles of the barn drummed almost deafeningly with relentless rainfall. "Hopefully it'll let up by morning."

"Come on, Balaam. Let's get you settled." The black man took the mule's reins and led him toward a stable. The animal's nostrils flared and it shied away, backing toward the double doors. In turn, Brimstone stood stone still, its dark muscles taut. The Morgan's eyes ignited with an otherworldly heat and it growled deeply in the back of its gullet.

"What's gotten into them?" asked the gunfighter.

Job stood where he was, peering into the deepening darkness that cloaked the stables. He fished the pocket watch from his vest and consulted the time. "I'd say in about ten minutes dusk will bleed into nightfall. That doesn't give us much time."

"I'm not following you. Time for *what*?"

Job studied the behavior of the horse and the mule. "Do me a favor. Walk along those stalls and take a look. Put that confounded glowing eye of yours to good use."

Dead-Eye nodded and shucked his pistol from its holster. He left the circle of light that the lantern provided and stepped into the darkness of the stable. The foxfire of his blind eye cast a muted glow ahead him, illuminating the earthen floor and the six stalls, three to the right and three to the left.

"Anything back there?"

The Southerner shrugged his narrow shoulders. "They're empty as far as I can tell. The floors are heavy with hay." He paused and listened. Abruptly, Dead-Eye recalled something from his former life…a snoring beneath the floorboards of a house. "Seems I hear breathing, though. Quite a bit of it. From the stalls and the hayloft."

Job listened to the storm rage outside. The structure around them creaked and groaned as the wind gained momentum. A moment later, the heavy rainfall turned into hail. The nuggets of ice struck the roof overhead like an unrelenting shower of stones.

"Get your ass over here and let's prepare ourselves," Job told him. "From the sound of the weather outside, we ain't going nowhere. So we're gonna have to stay put and stand our ground."

Dead-Eye nodded and joined Job where he, Brimstone, and Balaam stood near the double doors. Knowing he must empty his pistol of the rounds it held, he raised the gun overhead and unleashed six rounds. Almost instantly, the bullet holes in the roof began to leak and spatter them with cold rain.

"Sakes alive!" proclaimed Job. "What a saphead move that was!"

"Just shut your yap and load that pepperbox of yours," grumbled Dead-Eye. One after another, he took six paper cartridges from his coat pocket, bit the ends off with his teeth, and loaded the chambers of the Dragoon with powder and wooden bullet, then packed the charges tightly with the hinged ram-pin beneath the barrel. He dislodged the spent percussion caps from the firing nipples and replaced them with fresh ones. He returned the revolver to its holster for the time being and swept the folds of his frock coat aside. He lifted the sawed-off shotgun from where it hung on its sling and cracked the breech. Removing the twelve-gauge shells, he replaced them with the ash wood loads Job had fashioned for him the night before.

He had scarcely snapped the gun shut, when a savage cry rang out from overhead. It was a fearful sound; a cross between a bobcat and a female gone insane. Dead-Eye lifted his gaze toward the hayloft and saw a woman dressed in a gingham dress and white apron leaping through the air toward him. Her homely face was as pale as lard, her eyes as red as freshly-let blood, and her mouth bristled with fangs sharp enough to cleave meat from the bone.

Dead-Eye tilted the scattergun upward from the hip, thumbed a single hammer, and fired. The load of ash wood caught her in the chest and lodged in her heart. Her shriek of triumph faded into a whimpering cry of defeat. He watched as her body began to shrivel and curl into itself, and exploded into a burst of dust and ash as it hit the earthen floor.

A bellow came from the direction of the stable. Dead-Eye turned to find a Holstein cow bursting through a stall door, flinging straw and splintered wood in its wake. The animal's eyes were milky white and its yellowed fangs jutted haphazardly from its upper and lower jaws. As it charged, Dead-Eye swung the scattergun around and unleashed the second load. He had been aiming for the bovine's forehead, but it slung and tossed its massive head, causing the plug of ash wood to hit its broad shoulder instead. The wound smoked and sizzled as the projectile penetrated the cow's hide and buried itself deep into putrid, bloodless muscle. The creature didn't falter, however. It lowered its head and came right on coming.

Before Dead-Eye could react and draw the Dragoon, a lithe, black shadow leapt over his head, planting itself between him and the rampaging beast. Brimstone reared on his back legs, eyes aglow and nostrils blowing bellows of sulfurous smoke and cinder. He brought his front hooves down upon the cow's head with such force that they brought the animal down in its tracks. Its head plowed into the earth of the barn floor as Brimstone's steel shoes—now white hot from the Hell that lived within—crushed the thick bones of the skull and mangled its cold, worm-ridden brain.

The gunfighter looked over to see that a flock of vampiric chickens were flying down out of the loft with the intention of attacking Job. The mojo man dispatched them, one by one, with wooden slugs from his pepperbox pistol. Before they could hit the ground, each one exploded in a flash of blue flame and dust, leaving a flurry of feathers in their place.

"Watch out!" Job hollered. "Behind you!"

Dead-Eye whirled to find that a large sow—at least three hundred pounds in weight—was galloping down the aisle between the stalls. The swine was bloated with decay, its snout and fanged mouth crawling with maggots. But it was fleet of foot and determined to reach the Southerner, no matter what might lay between them. It jumped atop the prone form of the mangled cow, then sprang upon its shoulders and launched itself into the air, aiming to dodge the demon in horseflesh. Brimstone was having none of it, though. He snapped out with teeth laced with crimson fire and latched onto one of the hog's rear legs. The Morgan slung the critter around with a strength beyond any that a normal horse would possess, then released him. It crashed into the barn wall with such force that it snapped the sow's spine and crushed its ribcage. But it refused to relinquish its desire for human blood. It sluggishly pulled itself toward the zombie with its front feet, its curved tusks gnashing and grating one against the other.

Dead-Eye drew his .44 and put three wooden slugs between the swine's tiny white eyes. It gave out a shrill squeal and collapsed in upon itself. Soon, only gray dust and squirming maggots marked the spot where it had once lain.

"Misery and murderation!" shouted Job.

Dead-Eye looked back in the black man's direction. A tall, lanky farmer with blood-stained overalls and chambray shirt had jumped down from the loft and was coming for the swamp magician. His hands were curled into bony claws and his eyes were hungry for the warm sustenance that only an open vein could provide. The gunfighter lifted his pistol into line, but found that he had no chance to fire.

Job whirled, taking a four-pronged pitchfork from where it hung on the barn wall. He spun and planted the jagged tines though the vampire's abdomen, just beneath the ribcage. The prongs emerged through the fiend's back and anchored into the rungs of the hayloft ladder, securing him there. Then Job took one of the ash wood stakes from his belt and, with all his might, buried it squarely into the breastbone of the undead sodbuster. Balaam delivered the fatal blow, kicking out with his back legs and striking the end of the stake, driving it deep within the bloodsucker's heart, like a ten-pound sledge anchoring a railroad spike into rocky hardpan.

Dead-Eye and Job watched grimly as the man's pale flesh withered and flaked away, leaving only scorched bones hanging from the prongs of the pitchfork. A moment more and the skeleton fissured and crumbled as well. Soon, the hayfork remained alone, anchored deeply into a rung of the ladder. The dust and refuse that had once been a hardworking man swirled in a lingering dust devil for a second or two, then fell and mingled with the earth and manure that made up the barn's floor.

"Is that all of them?" the black man wondered aloud.

"I reckon not," said Dead-Eye. He spotted two red-eyed rats running along an overhead beam and plugged both with a fan of the hammer. Then he whirled at the furious flapping of wings to find a monstrous barn owl swooping down upon his head. He ducked as it clutched at his head with its razored talons and, thankfully, only lost his hat to the bird's fury. He lifted the big Colt and fired his final shot. The whittled bullet of ash tunneled through the owl's ass-end, angling up through its innards, and ending up in its biscuit-sized brain. It veered sharply in its flight, dropping the black hat, and slamming, face-first into the double-doors. Like the chickens, it burst into blue flame and a cloud of dust, then dissipated as it drifted earthward.

Dead-Eye shook his head and bent down to retrieve his hat. "Next time we'll take our chances at getting lightning-struck." Curiously, he looked over at Job. "Did Jules Holland turn all these? If so, he had an all-powerful thirst."

The mojo man studied the gray ash that lay scattered across the barn floor. "More than likely, no. He probably feasted on the farmer and his wife, but the critters probably came about when the two set about in search of sustenance. One fed upon the other until a whole passel of vampires were created and took refuge in this here barn."

"Damn," said the zombie. "Do you realize what could happen over a matter of years? This curse could spread far and wide, infect half the nation before it could be put to an end."

"That's why we've gotta ride fast in the morning," Job told him. "From what we've heard from folks, they can't be more than a day's ride or two ahead of us. I'm willing to travel day and night to catch up to 'em."

"I have no need for sleep," said Dead-Eye, "and neither does Brimstone. But you and Balaam…"

"Don't worry about us. Balaam is a tough, old ass. And so am I."

The gunslinger's smile was practically skeletal in nature. "Well, you're certainly an ass, that's for sure."

Job shook his head. "Keep that ghoulish grin to yourself. It gave me gooseflesh just looking upon it."

Something crossed Dead-Eye's mind. "You don't figure this was a trap, do you? Evangeline couldn't have conjured this storm to drive us in here, could she?"

"I wouldn't put anything past her. She's got so many tricks up her sleeve, there's no telling what she might do." Job glanced around the barn. He could tell by the mule's behavior that the danger had passed. There was nothing more to fear within the four walls. "Let's round up some oats and alfalfa for Balaam. Brimstone's belly oughta be full from that possum he ate a mile or two back down the trail. After that, we'll settle them in for the night."

"Then what?"

"Then we get to work," the mojo man told him. "You'll build a fire and stoke it hot. I'll fetch my melting pot, bullet mold, and silverware...and we'll set off at first light tomorrow, loaded for bear."

CHAPTER TWELVE

Along a Lonesome Road near Lynchburg, Tennessee
Late-October 1866

For a day and half they rode, stopping only to eat, and water and feed their mounts. Brimstone seemed as tireless and unaffected by lack of rest and slumber as his deceased master. The demon-horse led the way, taking point. Dead-Eye studied the trail ahead of them, looking for signs of the outlaws' passing. Every now and then, they would happen across a scene of deliberate cruelty and brutality, and they knew Holland and his followers had, indeed, traveled that way. Sometimes it was a single victim, while other times it was the savaging of many, reminiscent of the church where time had stood still, but not nearly as restrained and merciful in nature.

Several times, they passed a graveyard and found one or more caskets being lowered into freshly-turned sod. The mourners would see them approach and either run for cover in fear or react threateningly, drawing their guns, as though letting the gunfighter and mojo man know, in no uncertain terms, that they were unwelcome.

When that happened, Dead-Eye and Job failed to even slow their pace. They rode past, perhaps swifter than before, and left the townsfolk to indulge in their grief and scorn.

An hour past noon on the second day, the two were traveling a desolate stretch of road that cut through miles of heavy forest, when they abruptly found themselves facing an obstacle that they could have never anticipated, let alone prepared for.

The woodland sounds around them—the rustle of a gentle breeze through autumn leaves, the sassy call of a jay, the trickling flow of a nearby brook—all seemed to hush suddenly and unexpectedly. Their mounts slowed their pace and snorted from their nostrils, as though hesitant to proceed.

Job reined the white mule to a halt. He sat in the saddle and inhaled deeply. "Do you smell that?"

Dead-Eye nodded. "What is it?"

"It's a number of things," he said, clearly disturbed. "The smell of fired pistols and freshly-let blood at a back room gambling table. The reek of degradation and death in an opium den. The stink of a whorehouse bedroom on a hot July afternoon. And there are other things, familiar, yet strange to the nostrils. Fire and cinder that have burned a thousand years or more. The sweat, tears, and regret of the damned, the musky odor of creatures unknown, and the nasty breath of some great beast that has feasted upon the dead and still has decaying meat and thickened blood clinging to its teeth." He looked over at the gunfighter. "And what do you make of it?"

Dead-Eye's face was solemn and still. "It is the stench of war," he told him. "The bitterness of gunpowder expended for hours upon end, from the muzzle of a musket or the barrel of a cannon. The foulness of limbs black and bloated with gangrene and infection upon a surgeon's table. The stench of the bloated bodies of soldiers defeated and forgotten, left to rot on the battlefield, their flesh torn asunder by buzzards and their eyes pecked away by crows."

"Yes. All of those things. And others from places we can only imagine." Job looked around steadily. "But where is it coming from?"

Dead-Eye nodded down the road a piece. "There."

They sat in their saddles and puzzled over what they were looking at. About fifty feet away, there was a small oval of black, just hanging there in mid-air. Its edges shimmered and sparkled with blue-white fire, like sparks cast off by the braking wheels of a train against steel rails. Inside the oval was pitch blackness. As the opening spun and stretched, increasing from a foot in width to fairly the length and width of a grown man, they could see it was not total darkness at all. Weaved among the tapestry of ebony were swirls of color and brilliant points of light, like the heavenly stars, but much older and more foreboding than any they had ever laid eyes on. A sensation swept over them, or rather, a combination of many. Frigid cold and searing heat. The shiver of fear and the premonition of heart-sinking dread. A soul-numbing heaviness like disastrous expectation; one that promised danger and disaster, mournful grief and tremendous loss the likes of which neither had come to experience during their lifetime.

"What the hell is it?" asked Job.

Dead-Eye stared at it and he knew. "It's the Hole out of Nowhere," he said, recalling Elmer Bradley's dying words.

The portal hung there for a long moment, then something appeared within the depths of its hollow. At first, Dead-Eye feared it was the thing called Mymahthu…the creature that had ensnared and fed upon the U.S. Marshal and his deputies. But as the form stepped from the hole, it turned out to be no monster at all. Or, at least, that was the initial impression it gave.

It was a man; tall in stature, lean of muscle, and deeply tanned. His face was handsome and clean-shaven, and his raven black hair was long and pulled back over his shoulders. He wore denim britches and a sleeveless vest, and his knee-high boots were of a peculiar pattern of hide that neither Job nor Dead-Eye could easily identify. Above the lapels of the vest, his upper chest was bare, as were both arms. Along the length of the stranger's right arm, from shoulder to fingertips, was an elaborate and disturbing tattoo that made the appendage resemble a dark green viper. Shiny eyes were etched upon the knobs of his knuckles and Dead-Eye swore they blinked and narrowed in contempt as he flexed the fingers of his hand. Strapped across his narrow hips was a double-holstered gun belt cradling two oddly-shaped pistols. The revolvers seemed to glow a muted red, like irons hot and ready for branding. His left hand held an equally peculiar rifle. It was long and smoldering hot with four barrels jutting from its breech rather than one. The stock and foregrip were of polished horn or bone and were engraved with archaic symbols that the Southerner was completely unfamiliar with.

"Who are you?" the mojo man asked boldly.

The stranger smiled easily with a humor that was both engaging and vaguely menacing at the same time. His eyes flashed like furnace coals within the shadow of his hat brim and his strong, white teeth seemed to glow from the inside out, as though their hollows were lit with flickering flame.

"I am Legion," he answered. "John Legion." His eyes danced wryly with mischief and malice. "And we are many."

"Did the witch, the one named Evangeline, conjure you and the hole you climbed out of?" asked Dead-Eye.

Legion laughed. "No one conjures me. I move back and forth, to and fro, between the Thresholds of my own accord. Let us just say that the sorceress and I...well, we are of the same *alliance.*"

"What manner of being are you?" Job asked him. "A demon?"

Again, John Legion laughed. "Some have called me such. I have been known as many things between this realm and that. But mostly I hunt and obtain the prizes that my clients value the most. And Miss Evangeline is one such patron of my services."

"So you're a lowdown bounty hunter?" asked Dead-Eye.

"Yes, in a manner of speaking."

"And she knows who we are?" asked Job with an expression of apprehension on his dark face.

"She knows that *someone* has been following her and her companions," Legion allowed. "But she is, presently, blind to your identities. She possesses the gift of precognition and sensed that two men pursued them relentlessly, but that is all that came to her."

"How much of a bounty has she offered you?"

Legion canted the unholy rifle across his bare shoulder. The scalding hot barrels sizzled and cooked the flesh underneath, but the tall man seemed not to notice. "Gold and silver hold no appeal for me. I do my bartering in souls. When the parasite Holland syphons blood and life from his victims, they return later, but the essence of their souls do not. Those are normally claimed by God or Lucifer for their separate dominions, but Evangeline has cheated them of their loot and kept them for her own. To assure that her and her fellow travelers are protected from undue harm, she is willing to impart a generous share to me. In the place I come from, human souls are like poker chips at a riverboat gambling table, but of considerable value. Infinitely precious, with the promise of great fortune."

"Are you aiming to kill us and make off with ours?" asked Job.

The bounty hunter's blazing eyes squinted until they were nothing more than flickering slits. It was as though he were looking past their skin and muscle, assessing what was housed inside.

"Yours is a bit worse for wear, but ripe for the picking, mojo man," said Legion, running his tongue along the edges of his incandescent teeth. He frowned when it came to Dead-Eye. "You...you shouldn't have one at all, given your present state of being. But it's there. Not the same as it was before, though. Now it is as black as the cloak of Death himself and pissed to no end."

"It isn't any wonder," said the corpse, "considering how I was tortured and killed."

A sly curiosity crossed John Legion's face. "Exactly who are you? And why do you loathe Holland and the others so?"

Dead-Eye nearly told Legion of his abducted son and his incessant desire for revenge, but he refrained from doing so. The less the bounty hunter and Holland's entourage knew about them, the better. "I was a fool," he said instead, swinging down out of his saddle and facing the man. "But no more. So, what are your intentions?"

"What they always are. Desecrate you and claim your souls for my own. Then I'll toss your severed heads at Evangeline's feet. She aims to hollow them out and hang them on the eaves of her wagon for lanterns."

"Well, if you've got a mind to kill us, you'd best commence to trying. 'Cause you've wasted enough of our time already."

John Legion smiled and bowed his head almost respectfully. Then, without warning, the strange rifle dropped down off his shoulder, the foregrip of polished bone falling into the palm of his left hand. The four barrels discharged instantly. Tongues of red fire belched from the muzzles...but it wasn't bullets that he was firing.

Instead, pliant balls of living flesh spun and opened as they were propelled forward. They unfolded into angry rattlesnakes. But they were like none that Dead-Eye or Job had ever encountered before. Their diamond-patterned hides were violet in color and, from their backs, arched wings of pale green membrane and angular bone. The four took flight like misshapen bats, soaring and swooping menacingly overhead.

Dead-Eye swung the sawed-down scattergun from beneath his coat and unleashed both barrels. Two of the flying serpents burst into fragments beneath a hail of double-aught buckshot. Six sections of squirming purple sidewinder hit the earth of the road, bucking and squirming, spouting jets of venomous green blood.

One of the flying snakes dived at Job's head as he sat in Balaam's saddle. The knife dropped from his sleeve, sliding smoothly into his grasp. He lashed out and sliced the viper cleanly in half. As the fourth went for the mule's haunches, Brimstone snapped out with his teeth and caught it in mid-air. It neglected to mangle his prey, choosing to swallow it whole instead.

The mojo man left his mount and stood looking down at the two pieces of the snake he had cleaved in two. He was shocked to find the head-end of the creature sprouting a new tail, rattles and all, while the tail end formed an upper portion. It regenerated swiftly, until the triangular head emerged, fully-formed, its mouth stretched wide, spurting poison from the hollows of its fangs.

"Don't cut 'em in half!" he hollered to Dead-Eye. "If you do, they'll sprout into two more. They're like Hydra. In case you don't know what that is, it's…"

"I'm an educated man, dammit!" the Southerner snapped. He watched as the six pieces of snakes he had blasted out the sky quickly changed into whole creatures of the same number. "It's that ornery nine-headed critter from Greek legend."

The two snakes that had sprang from one, struck at the mojo man's ankles, but he danced away swiftly, dodging their fangs. "Balaam!" the black man shouted. "Take care of these slithery little bastards!"

Without hesitation, the mule leapt and planted its hooves forcefully upon the back of the serpent on the right. Fire flashed from beneath the animal's feet and the violet snake with the flapping, green wings began to blacken and curl into a smoldering, dry husk. Balaam pounced again, nailing the second rattler as well, bringing about another flaming demise.

"How did he do that?" asked Dead-Eye.

"Old Balaam is prepared for such," the swamp wizard told him. "His shoes are cast of solid silver."

"Now you tell me!" grumbled the gunfighter. He stepped back swiftly as the six serpents at his feet completed their transformations and prepared to take flight. Dead-Eye drew the Dragoon swifter than the eye could follow and unleashed six shots with the fanning of his palm. A half dozen silver bullets drilled the thickening bodies of the vipers, defeating them with the same taint of precious metal that the mule's horseshoes had delivered. Each one ignited and was soon no more than piles of bone and cinder.

Job eyed John Legion cautiously. "Quite some ammunition you came packing," he told him. "Apparently the critters you harbor from your dominion are as backasswards as you are."

The bounty hunter laughed. "I acquire the tools of my trade from realm to realm, one place in time to the other. Believe it or not, these came from *your* world…from a distant time known as the Burn. A time when something infinitely more destructive than gunpowder could destroy cities and towns, forests and mountains in the wink of an eye. It was a world abundant with evil with very little good to be found. These things you defeated, they were mutations…a product of the Burn. I just took them back with me and, with the help of an alchemist, formed them into the way they are now." Resentment shown in his handsome face. "Or, rather, *were.*"

The zombie's blind eye glowed from the shade of his hat brim as he glared at the bounty hunter. "Enough of history lessons and idle talk," he said. "If we're gonna end this, let's get on with it."

"Of course…but you are at a disadvantage, are you not?"

"How so?"

Legion shook his head, as though he was in the presence of a complete imbecile. "What do you have to face me with? An empty shotgun and an equally impotent six-gun. No more silver to battle the unholy with."

Dead-Eye knew he was right. He was in a precarious predicament.

"So, it is my turn to draw." And he did, with speed and accuracy. He drew one of the red-hot pistols from its holster and fired from the hip.

The projectile struck Dead-Eye squarely in the stomach, rocking him back a couple of steps. He glanced over at Job, as if saying *What a shit-brained halfwit!* But the uneasy look in the black man's eyes told him that he wasn't at all sure that was the case.

The gunslinger turned back to the one who had shot him. "I'm already dead, simpleton. Bullets can't harm me."

John Legion flashed that wolfish grin of his. "You're correct. But, regrettably for you, that wasn't a bullet at all."

Suddenly, Dead-Eye felt a bizarre sensation take hold of his guts. There was a moist *pop* as the fiery gun's projectile ruptured—or *hatched*—and something began to writhe and squirm within his abdomen. Soon, the invader within him began to grow at an alarming rate, displacing his organs and causing the pale flesh of his belly to swell, like a woman with child. He felt no pain, but was alarmed at what was taking place, for he knew its fruition would not be in his favor.

"Good God Almighty!" exclaimed Job, his eyes widening in horror.

The flesh of Dead-Eye's stomach split open and the silk material of his shirt ripped apart. He watched, astounded, as the blunted head of a large serpent emerged from his guts and looked around, as if in curiosity. Tissue rended and bones crackled as the body of the snake became too much for the zombie's lanky frame to accommodate. The sheer weight of the creature drove Dead-Eye to his knees. It slithered from the hole—covered with congealed blood and shit from the gunfighter's ruptured bowels—and crawled on its belly into the roadway.

"What the hell is this thing?" asked Dead-Eye, a bit embarrassed that his entrails were hanging out, trailing from one direction to the other.

"It's a boa," Job told him. He took a few steps backwards as the serpent spotted him and began slithering in his direction. "I've seen them in the far reaches of the bayou. They don't grow nearly as big and as fast as this one, however!"

As the snake came for him, it seemed to grow larger with each passing moment. When it had left Dead-Eye's body, it had been six or seven feet in length. But as it came within twenty feet of him, it had lengthened to nearly eighteen. And it was pert near as thick around as a telegraph pole.

"No need to take off running," John Legion told him. "It'll catch up to you before you can get ten steps. Then it'll crush your bones and swallow you whole. I'll have that head of yours before you're all the way down its gullet…and that tarnished soul of yours for my treasure purse."

But, surprisingly enough, the mojo man seemed to have no intention of fleeing. He stood his ground, scratching his stubbled cheek and studying the advancing serpent sagely. He also noticed, further on, that Dead-Eye was digging in his coat pocket for something.

The boa—now nearly as long as a Conestoga wagon and a team of horses—was only ten feet away, when Job acted. He jerked one of the tiny glass bottles—the red one—off its lanyard. Crushing it between his fingers, he flung the contents at the creature. The powder was drawn to the snake's lengthy body like metal filings to magnetite, coating the scales, then sinking past them into the meat underneath. The boa's muscles begin to knot up and convulse, and its unnaturally red eyes rolled upward into its long skull until the slitted pupils had vanished from view. Job then lifted the shriveled chicken foot on his chain and began to circle the thrashing snake, chanting something inexplicable in a low, sing-song tone of voice. Slowly, the dirt of the road lifted upward in an earthy swirl, engulfing the reptile and obscuring its quivering body from view.

Midway through the ritual, Job glanced over at the tall man with the serpent tattoo. John Legion looked bewildered, as if wondering what the black man was up to. Then, on the seventh circling of the cloud, the dust gently settled. The giant snake was gone. In its place was an earthworm. Before anyone could react, a hawk soared down from an oak branch nearby, scooped the worm up in its talons, and sailed off through the treetops.

"It seems that you are just as powerful as the witch...maybe even more so," Legion allowed. He lifted his pistol at arm's length and aimed it squarely at Job. "But I've come to do a job and now it is time to finish it. Let us see how good you are at conjuring with an egg hatching in your throat. More than likely, it will rip your head clean off trying to get out and I'll have both my prizes in hand."

Before the bounty hunter could pull the trigger, however, another shot rang out. John Legion flinched at the boom, jerking his head sharply to the left. He didn't escape entirely unscathed, however. A silver slug furrowed the flesh of his right cheek. It moved diagonally, starting at the corner of his mouth and traveled past his cheekbone, then punched an opening as clean as a buttonhole in the lobe of his ear. The man's tanned flesh popped and sizzled, casting off curls of noxious blue smoke. Although he failed to cry out, Legion grimaced in pain. He glared at Dead-Eye, who had reloaded with a paper cartridge from his pocket when he had been distracted by Job's voodoo ritual.

The mojo man drew the pepperbox pistol from his vest and aimed it at Legion. His hand was as steady as a frozen pump handle on a snowy January morning. "You'd best get your sorry ass back in that hole and git," he warned. "'Cause the next shot or two are going square betwixt those smart-alecky eyes of yours. And it'll be your goldang head bobbing from the horn of my saddle."

Slowly, John Legion returned the strange pistol to its holster and backed toward the oval portal behind him. "Don't trick yourself into believing that this is over and done with," he warned the two. "Once

I take a job, I don't rest easy 'til it's finished and the bounty is paid in full."

"I said what I meant." Job cocked his piece, cycling the long, six-chambered cylinder for the first shot. "Get back to the hell you came from."

Legion raised a hand to his cheek and probed the ugly wound in the side of his face. He scowled hatefully at the lanky gunfighter and the mojo man, then stepped reluctantly back through the portal. He soon merged with the darkness beyond and was gone. Gradually, the hole in the air shortened and narrowed. Then, with a crackle of sparks, it was gone. All that was left as evidence of the bounty hunter's being there were the blackened mounds where the winged rattlesnakes had shriveled and burnt.

"'Twas quite a bluff you pulled there," said Dead-Eye, still on his knees. "I know for a fact that pistol isn't loaded with silver. You didn't even possess a mold of that caliber."

Job returned the pepperbox to his vest and removed his derby hat, blotting beads of sweat from his brow with a handkerchief he produced from his britches pocket. "I'm just glad you got that one shot loaded and fired. If not, there wouldn't have been no bluffing to it a'tall."

Dead-Eye looked mournfully down at his intestines, lying about in the dust of the roadway. "I'm all unraveled," he said. "Think you could reload these innards and stitch me up again?"

The mojo cussed as he set the bowler back atop his bald head and started for the pack mule. "Hellfire and damnation! There goes my dad-blasted fiddle strings again!"

CHAPTER THIRTEEN

On the Banks of the Mississippi River
November 1866

For another day and night they rode, relentlessly, knowing they had little time for food or rest. Brimstone was like a hound dog when it came to catching scent and following track, and he soon closed the gap between them and the band of nefarious outlaws.

Dead-Eye sat tall in the saddle, his forty-four packed with alternate loads of ash wood and silver. He grumbled and growled about the shirt the boa constrictor had ruined during its birthing, vowing to buy another garment when they reached the next dry goods store.

Job sat perched atop Balaam a yard or so behind the gunfighter. The white mule followed the Morgan's lead, none too happy about the next danger that might present itself, but resigned to facing it, nevertheless. The mojo man smoked his pipe and pondered the conflict that lay ahead. Every now and then, he would fish the spell book from his vest pocket and flip through the pages, seeking hexes and incantations that might give them an edge when they confronted Jules Holland, Evangeline, and the unholy three.

When they reached the town of Dyersburg, they knew they were on the right track. The citizens cowered behind shuttered windows and locked doors, distrustful of any stranger who appeared on the main thoroughfare. Dead-Eye and Job failed to understand their fear and suspicion, until they reached the far end of town. There, a church—Roman Catholic in denomination—had been burnt until only the frame of blackened timbers remained. From the center beam within the structure hung four bodies from lengths of scorched hemp. One was a priest, while the others were nuns. Their vestments and habits had been ignited and singed away, leaving only their decimated bodies nearly burnt to the bone. Around the charred pulpit, pages from an ancient Bible had been ripped from their binding and defecated upon.

They sat in their saddles for a long moment and grimly observed the blasphemous ruination that the parish had been subjected to. Job removed his hat and held it to his breast in reverence. Dead-Eye simply glared at what had been done there, wantonly and needlessly, more than likely for no reason at all.

"Once we catch up with these fiends…then what?" he asked his companion. "Do you have a plan in mind?"

Job shrugged his skinny shoulders. "I reckon you'll take on Holland and the three, and I'll face Evangeline. Brimstone and Balaam will do what they can, of that I'm sure. Our main concern, of course, is the boy."

"Daniel," said the dead man.

"Yes, Daniel. We must ensure that he is not harmed in any way, either by the others…or by us, as the fighting commences."

Dead-Eye turned in his saddle and regarded the mojo man, face to face. "Tell me…do we have a chance? To prevail against such evil and depravity? Or are we bound to be defeated?"

"That could very well be," Job told him. "But we've got to try at least, don't we? That is why you were murdered in the first place…because you had the nerve to face the unknown and the impossible. Now you are armed with skills and advantages you lacked before. Immortality, a swift gun hand, and no inhibition or fear whatsoever. Me? I've got my spells and charms and decades of hoodoo knowledge. Hopefully, betwixt the two of us, it'll be enough to bring an end to them and the madness they've wrought across this land."

The following morning found them riding across a broad pasture. Dead corn stalks had been tented and tied together, and the ground lay fallow and devoid of the fruits of the harvest. Beyond the field was a line of tall trees; cedar, birch, and long-leaved pine.

Job reined the white mule to a halt and held his hand up. "Stop and listen!"

Dead-Eye did as he said. Up ahead, they could hear the roaring of water.

"We've reached the river."

"Yes." The mojo man spurred his mount, urging it into a gallop. "Let's go!"

Together, the two rode across the acreage and reached the tree line. The thicket around the base of the trunks was thick and treacherous, but they pushed their way through and soon found themselves upon the banks of the broad waterway that separated the eastern territory from the west.

For a long moment, they could do nothing more than sit there and stare in dread and dismay.

"Well," said Dead-Eye. "I reckon we'll have to change its name from the mighty Mississippi to the River Nile."

Job stared at the rushing currents that coursed between the two banks. Muddy water no longer surged through the deep channel. Instead, it was filled with the rich crimson of fresh blood.

"Lord help us," hissed the black man beneath his breath. He closed his eyes and shook his head sadly. "I'll be damned if her mama didn't teach her well."

Dead-Eye looked over at his fellow rider "Give it to me straight, Job. Just who the hell is this woman?"

A weary and sorrowful expression creased the mojo man's dark face, causing it to appear twenty years older than it had the day before.

"The witch...Evangeline." Job stared forlornly across the sanguine river, as though he were looking through the open gates of Hell itself. "She is my daughter."

TO BE CONTINUED...

ABOUT THE AUTHOR

Born and bred in Tennessee, **Ronald Kelly** has been an author of Southern-Fried horror fiction for 35 years, with fifteen novels, twelve short story collections, and a Grammy-nominated audio collection to his credit. Influenced by such writers as Stephen King, Ray Bradbury, Richard Matheson, Joe R. Lansdale, and Manly Wade Wellman, Kelly sets his tales of rural darkness in the hills and hollows of his native state and other locales of the American South. His published works include *Fear, Undertaker's Moon, Blood Kin, Hell Hollow, Hindsight, The Buzzard Zone, After the Burn, Midnight Grinding, Mister Glow-Bones, The Halloween Store, Season's Creepings, Irish Gothic,* and *The Web of La Sanguinaire & Other Arachnid Horrors.* His Silver Shamrock collection of extreme horror tales, *The Essential Sick Stuff,* won the 2021 Splatterpunk Award for Best Collection. Kelly lives in a backwoods hollow in Brush Creek, Tennessee with his wife and young'uns.

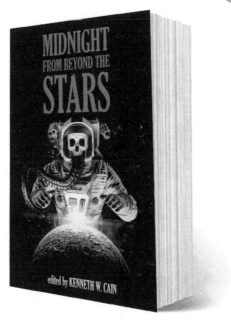

To escape her fanatically religious upbringing, Mia moves away to attend State University instead of the bible-college her family wanted. After orientation, Mia's new friends invite her to the Para-Psychology Club, where she meets a charismatic professor, who introduces her to Astral Projection. Mia finds that her social anxiety makes her a natural at the maneuver. So, when her possessive boyfriend tracks her down, hellbent on returning her home, she escapes their possessive grip by slipping into the nether. However, while out of her body, something ancient and dark—and from her past—takes over. Forced to deal with not only the entity now using her body but also the religious extremists who have arrived to remove it, her only hope lies in the hands of her new friend Bruce and the enigmatic Professor Colista as they try to save her from a fate beyond hell.

Made in the USA
Columbia, SC
23 December 2021

51708349R00093